The Wake

Books by Steve Allen

BOP FABLES   1955
FOURTEEN FOR TONIGHT   1955
THE FUNNY MEN   1956
WRY ON THE ROCKS   1956
THE GIRLS ON THE 10TH FLOOR   1958
THE QUESTION MAN   1959
MARK IT AND STRIKE IT   1960
NOT ALL OF YOUR LAUGHTER,
NOT ALL OF YOUR TEARS   1962
LETTER TO A CONSERVATIVE   1965
THE GROUND IS OUR TABLE   1966
BIGGER THAN A BREADBOX   1967
A FLASH OF SWALLOWS   1969
THE WAKE   1972

The Wake

STEVE ALLEN

DOUBLEDAY & COMPANY, INC., GARDEN CITY, NEW YORK

1972

ISBN: 0-385-07608-8
Library of Congress Catalog Card Number 72–83136

To the Donahues who, despite their tragedies,
rarely complained.

The Wake

CHAPTER ONE

David Considine lay half awake, thinking that the moment when you first slid up out of sleep was one of the best he knew. It was not good if you awakened cold, with the covers off, or if you awakened too late and had to rush up and about before you were really ready to. But when you could just lie in bed, coming to slowly, it was beautiful. Especially if, off in another part of the house, you could hear the voices of the grownups.

Sometimes, when he awakened, for a few seconds he did not know where he was. He would think he was in New York with his mother and then discover that he was only in Chicago with Aunt Mag and Grandma Scanlan. Or he would think that he was with Aunt Mag and then awaken to find that he was in a boarding-school cot, in a large room with other children he scarcely knew. Or he would believe he was at Grandma Considine's place, only to realize, upon attaining a slightly higher level of consciousness, that he was in another town, boarding for a while with a friend of the family. Except for the mornings he awakened, saddened, to know that he was not in a home at all but in a cold dormitory, it was not too bad. There was still the warmth of the

1

blankets, the softness of the mattress, perhaps the smell of bacon or burning toast, of coffee, which he liked to smell but not to drink, and the wonderful voices from the other rooms, the deep, gruff voices of his uncles, or the soft morning voices of the women.

When he did not have to hurry to school, on weekends, or during the hot Midwestern summers, he loved to lie in bed at such times, figuring out first where he was, then trying to identify the voices, if any, enjoying the aroma of breakfast being prepared. He saw things more clearly at such times and heard better, too. Casual sights and sounds that were of no interest once the day had started on its hectic course seemed somehow greatly fascinating. The rhythmic ticking of a clock, on rainy days the whish-waaasshh of tires in the street, the clip-clop of a passing milkman's or iceman's horse, even the pale thuds, creaks, hums and drippings, bumps and sighs that seemed made by the walls, floors and ceilings themselves were of interest.

It did not take much, at such times, to make simple existence on the earth seem somehow exciting, in a quiet way.

The best time of all was when the voices from elsewhere in the house, from another bedroom, from a kitchen, from a hallway, were talking about him. It did not matter a great deal what they were saying since they rarely if ever spoke of him in critical tones in his absence, although they were sometimes bitterly sharp to his face. But the soft morning compliments were more delicious than those heard at any other time.

"He's a good boy."

"He really put away a good meal, didn't he?"

"I wonder what he'll be when he grows up."

"When he came back from the store he gave me every penny of the change."

Any little remark made him feel positively wonderful.

The last few dreams of morning were in some strange way the better too. His favorite was the flying dream. Even wide-awake he was by no means entirely convinced that he could not possibly fly, so strong were the dream memories of soaring over vast valleys, alighting graceful as a bird on the fender of some enormous black Model-T Ford and using the tight curved metal as a sort of diving board, to get a good spring-up back to higher air.

He knew that as of any waking moment his feet were hopelessly glued to the ground and yet it seemed that there had been a time, not terribly long before, when merely by the strength of will he'd decided to lift himself up into the air, slowly at first, flying rather low so as not to fight with fear as well as gravity simultaneously about the yard behind the apartment building, or higher then above the alleys of the neighborhood and then at last, ever higher, over the wide, green empty lots of the South Side of Chicago and after that no limits to his scope.

Now, well out of dreams of flying, comforted to know that he was wide-awake in bed, and not escaping whatever faceless monster had pursued him only moments before, he lay waking peacefully, looking up under the skirt of the morning as a moist breeze gently lifted the cheap lace curtains beside his bed. He was wondering why he did not feel like crying about his grandmother's death.

Perhaps it was just that at the age of eight you were not supposed to cry any more. But the main thing was: It did not seem real. He thought for a moment that if he just got up and walked into the kitchen the old lady would be there this morning as in the past, smiling at him distantly with her old, toothless mouth, lifting up the yellow window shades, saying as she frequently did, "The light of heaven to our poor souls," in her weary, absent-minded way.

The light in reality was the dusty gray glow that reflected from the blank brick wall of the building next door, the gray light that in a mysterious way seemed to have something to do with "the Depression." *Depression.* The kernel of the word was never revealed to David, but its outer husk was formidable enough. He knew that it had something to do with not getting enough spending money, uncles out of work, buildings boarded up with "Keep Out—This Means You" signs on them, something to do with wearing secondhand clothes sent to him by an older cousin who lived in Los Angeles.

He dimly remembered Los Angeles, a great endless green park, full of pretty houses and funny-looking trees that looked like the foliage in Tarzan movies. Chicago was dirty and tough but he preferred it because it was home, which meant that it was where Aunt Mag and Aunt Rose and Uncle Mike and Uncle Charlie and Grandma Scanlan lived. And sometimes Mama, when she was able to arrange it. It was where Lon Warneke pitched fast balls to Gabby Hartnett for the Cubs, and Al Simmons and Zeke Bonura hit home runs for the White Sox. He had all their pictures—and scores more—on bubble-gum baseball cards, piled up in a neat stack on his dresser.

In a gray casket in the parlor reposed the lifeless body of Bridget Scanlan, rich silver hair gleaming, hands folded across her stomach. The black rosary beads she had so often fondled, as she had rocked back and forth in her chair of creaky oak and stiff leatherette beside the enormous Majestic radio, were now clutched in her pale fingers. The sweet green smell of fern and rose filled the room and the light of a pair of enormous candles mingled with that of the early and chill September morning.

Two men, poorly dressed, carrying their gray tweed caps in rough workmen's hands, knelt before the casket in silent prayer. The shorter of the two, Tom Monaghan, wore a dark lumber jacket though his shoes had been well shined for the occasion. He felt only moderately sad at contemplation of the lifeless body before him, since he had seen the old woman but rarely in the last dozen years, but was present largely out of a sense of social obligation. The Scanlans had been well represented at the funeral of his own mother, only a year earlier, and it was chiefly of her that he now daydreamed rather than of Bridget Scanlan.

He felt vaguely pious, ill at ease, and sentimental on behalf of his good friends who had suffered such a loss. Of death itself he had seen more than enough, in the war in France. He had discovered two interesting things about himself in battle: that he was a coward, but fiercely courageous if he lost his temper. In his first exposure to shelling and through the first infantry charges up and out of the trenches, he had been weak with fear, sick as he saw his friends drop and then, in hand-to-hand combat with a German soldier who turned out to be little more than a boy, had suddenly become enraged when the man had swung a punch at him clumsily.

"Why, you son of a bitch!" he had shouted, retrieving his fallen rifle. Then he had killed the boy-man, and kicked at him as he lay in the mud, shouting obscenities. He had never entirely gotten over the surprise of discovering that he was something more than the genial if occasionally short-tempered Tommy Monaghan known to all his friends, that he was in fact, a murderer, if the occasion required. Not in the legal sense, God knows; it had been self-defense and all that, kill or be killed, but he had never thought the same of himself after the moment of that discovery.

At his side big John O'Toole wiped a tear from his eye with a clublike fist. He was genuinely sorrowful because of the passing of yet one more member of his mother's generation, of the old women who had left Ireland as young girls, coming to the wild, rough cities on the American continent. His own mother, dead a dozen years, had grown up on a farm, had come poor—like all the rest—to America on her honeymoon with the giant of a sailor she had married. Big John thought now of his sorrow that he had not learned more of his ancestry and history from these two soft-spoken immigrants. His father had told him one story, of the ill-fated

ship *Erin's Hope* that in April of 1867 had set sail secretly
out of New York Harbor, pretending to be on a casual ex-
cursion to Cuba but in reality bound for the West Coast of
Ireland to help the revolutionaries then fighting the British,
carrying arms disguised in wine barrels, piano crates and the
like. O'Toole's father had been in the harbor of Sligo a month
later when, not knowing all was already lost and the battle
over, the Irish-Americans had arrived at the end of their long
journey. O'Toole the elder had helped row a small boat out
to the ship to warn the visitors that their valiant effort had
been for naught and that even then British gunboats were
steaming toward Sligo to capture them. O'Toole had gone on
board, learned the details of the journey, and not left the
ship till its next stop, at a port some distance to the north.
Like so much of the history of Ireland the story was one of
ignorance, frustration and defeat. Of the larger canvas of
that history John O'Toole, this morning in 1931, knew next
to nothing, but the one story his father had told him had
fired him, at least during his younger days, with the dream
and hope that he might have participated, or might yet take
part, in some important adventure. Instead, his life in Chicago had been largely a matter of one plodding day after
another. The world seemed to be speeding past him but
from his own vantage point existence seemed slow and somehow sad and not very interesting. And all the old-timers from
Ireland were dead or dying.

At that moment, Margaret Scanlan, feeling particularly
middle-aged, emerged from a bedroom, looking down at her
dress as she completed buttoning it. She was surprised to

discover her older sister Josephine standing absently, looking out of the window.

"Josie," she said quietly, "what the hell did you do with my curling iron?"

"What?" Josie said.

"I could use my curling iron."

"You look as if you could use an iron lung," Josie said, "but I don't know where it is."

"You must know. Don't you remember? I gave it to you last night before we went to bed."

"Well, I don't know," Josie said, yawning. "I didn't sleep a wink." She stretched her arms out before her and cracked her knuckles. Then, moving toward the living room, Josie pointed to the visitors, unseen by them, after which she put her finger to her lips by way of warning her sister that strangers were present. The men were in reality not strangers at all but good friends of long standing. To the Scanlans, however, there was a sense in which everyone on earth not directly a member of the family was a stranger. The world was divided into Us and the Others. The others might now and then be trusted, even loved, but they would always be a breed apart.

When Tom Monaghan heard the two women approach behind him he rose stiffly to his feet, as did his companion.

"Ah, good mornin', Maggie," he said.

"How are ya, Tommy?" Margaret said, shaking his hand.

"You know John O'Toole," Monaghan said.

"Of course," Margaret said. "Josie, you know the—"

"Yes," Josie said. "I let them in a few minutes ago."

"We're sorry for your trouble, Mag," Tom Monaghan said. "Mighty sorry."

"Indeed we are," John O'Toole said. He was a head taller than Monaghan and a bit clumsy. "She was a fine old soul, as we were just sayin' to your sister."

"Thank you," Margaret said. "I know Ma thought the world of you both, too. It's good of yez to come."

"Well," Tom said, "I always said that Bridget Scanlan was one of the true saints on earth and the whole neighborhood'll miss her, believe me."

"Thank you," Margaret said. "Would you care for a cup of tea? Or coffee maybe, since it's so early in the mornin'?"

"Well, now," O'Toole mumbled, "we don't want to be puttin' you to any trouble now."

"It's no trouble at all," Margaret said. "I got the pot on in the kitchen. If you'd like go on in there and help yourselves. Just make yourselves at home and stay as long as you like."

"Fine, Mag," Monaghan said. "Come on, John. We'll have us a cup of java at that."

As they passed down the green-carpeted hallway toward the kitchen, out of earshot of the women, Monaghan added under his breath, "If Mike is home maybe we'll have somethin' a little stronger than coffee, eh, John?"

"I was just thinkin' the same thing meself," O'Toole said. "Jeez, I'd peddle the flag right now for the price of a drink."

Standing beside the coffin Margaret said, "Ma looks wonderful, doesn't she, Josie?"

"Yes," Josie said, weeping and blowing her nose. "Maggie, why didn't you let me know earlier how sick she was?"

"I didn't know myself, Josie, till just the last week or so. You know Ma. She was never one to complain."

"I know," Josie said. Then, with a bitter expression, she said, "Do you think Mike's drinking had anything to do with it?"

"Now, Josie," Margaret said, "don't start that. Mike's been on the wagon for about six weeks now. Ma worried about him all the time, of course, but sure she did that all her life, God knows."

"Where *is* he?" Josie asked.

Margaret moved a tall basket of flowers closer to the window.

"He'll be back in a little while," she said. "He said he wanted to get some air."

"Get some *beer* is more like it," Josie said, turning as she heard David enter.

"Aunt Mag," the boy called out, "is the coffin—?" He stopped as he saw the casket.

"Yes, honey. They brought it in last night. Go over and say a prayer for your poor grandma."

"All right." He did so, kneeling, head bowed.

"Josie," Margaret said, "where'd you put my curling iron?"

"I *told* you," Josie said. "I don't know." She yawned deeply and said, "God, I'm tired. I didn't sleep a wink last night."

"You didn't, huh?" Margaret said, tilting her head sarcastically.

"Not a wink."

"Well, then there must have been somebody else in bed with the two of us because *somebody* was snoring the whole damn night. You had poor Davey tossin' and turnin' on his cot all night with your noise."

"Aunt Josie," David said, rising, "why do we have to pray for Grandma?"

"What?" Josie said, sharply. "What kind of a question is that?"

"Well," David said, "she was such a *good* old lady, always sayin' the rosary and everything, and she never did anything bad at all so I'll bet she just went right to heaven and if she did, then why do we have to pray for her?"

"David," Josie said, "don't ask stupid questions."

"Josie, that's not a stupid question," Margaret interrupted. "It's a good question." She patted David's head, stroking his hair.

"You see, honey, you're right. We may be wastin' our time at that, but you can't be sure. Only God knows if Grandma went straight to heaven, so just to be on the safe side we say—you know—just a few 'Hail, Marys' for her. Just to be sure. Have you had your breakfast?"

"I didn't finish the oatmeal," he said, "but I ate three pieces of cinnamon toast. You sure make it good, Aunt Maggie. Is it okay if I go out and play?"

"I don't think," Josie said, "that on a day like this—"

"Sure, it'll be all right," Margaret said. "But don't get your nice clothes all mussed up, and don't make any noise outside, all right?"

"Okay," David said, turning.

"It's chilly out. Put on a sweater. The new one I got you."

"All right," David said, running to the bedroom.

"I don't think he ought to be out playing at a time like this," Josie said. "If he were mine I'd tell—"

"Well, he's not yours, Josie."

"And he's not yours, either. Where *is* Belle, by the way? Is she going to show up at all before poor Ma is in her grave at Mount Olivet?"

"Yes, she'll be here," Margaret said. "But you know Belle."

"I know her, all right," Josie said. "She'll probably—"

"Ssshhh!" Margaret cut in, pointing to David as he hurried back into the room and out the front door, pulling on a heavy sweater.

"Why isn't she here?" Josie said. "Always talking about how much she loves Ma—and she's not even here! Well, there's one thing. Poor Ma can see. She can look down now, Maggie, and see who loves her."

"Oh, Josie, what are ya talkin' about? We *all* loved her, and wherever she is she knows that's the God's truth."

"Then why isn't Belle here?"

"If you must know," Margaret said, turning away, "it's on account of *you.*"

"What?"

"I wasn't going to say anything, but I don't see how I can keep everything to myself all the time. Sometimes you all make me sick, with your jealousy and fighting and drinking."

"You've never seen me drunk in my life," Josie cried.

"Oh, I didn't mean you about the drink; that's all Rose and Belle and the boys, but the rest of it still goes. Here poor

Ma isn't dead two days and already there's trouble again."

"And is that supposed to be *my* fault?"

"No, I guess not," Margaret said, sighing. "Well, what happened is, Belle got in town last Monday and—"

"She's been here all week?" Josie cut in. "She was in town before Ma died?"

"Yes," Margaret said, starting to pace the floor nervously. "I sent her a wire the same time I sent the one to you in Los Angeles. She was playin' in St. Louis—I forget the theatre—anyway, she came on and then she called me Monday from the Union Station downtown and she said, 'Maggie, how is Ma?' And I said, 'Belle, Ma's dyin'.' And she said, 'No. She can't be dyin'. I'll move right in this morning and nurse her back to health.' And I said, 'Belle, you can't; there's no room.' Well, that's all she needed. She said, 'What do you *mean,* there's no room?' And I said, 'Josie got in yesterday and so there's no room. And you know anyway,' I said, 'that with the two of yez under the same roof there's always trouble.' And she said, 'Oh, I get it. It's all right for Ma to take my twenties and fifties and the hundreds I've been sending—my *money* is pretty Goddamned welcome,' she said, 'but *I'm* not, is that it?' Well, you know Belle. She said, 'Maggie, you tell Ma I love her, always have and always will and tell her I'll see her soon when she gets well and all. But first, by God,' she said, 'I'm gonna get stinkin' drunk and stay that way for a week.'"

"Oh, sure," Josie said. "She was just lookin' for an excuse."

"No, Josie. She said, 'I've been on the wagon for months,

but now, by God, if that's the way you're all going to treat me—then to hell with *all* of you.' "

"So where is she?"

"God knows. Rose checked a few of the hotels on the South Side where she sometimes stays when she and that Doug Roberts are in town. She *had* checked into one of them but the desk clerk said he hadn't seen her since the first night."

"I'm not surprised."

"Oh, Josie, poor Belle means well. And Ma's gone, so it's too late for that. Belle never got to see her in time, but that's over and done. What I'm worried about is Davey. He keeps sayin', 'Where's Mama Belle? Where's my mama?' and I don't know how long I can get away with lying to him."

A soft knock sounded at the front door.

"Oh, Josie," Margaret said, "I just remembered. I sent John O'Toole and Tom Monaghan down to the kitchen. You answer the door while I get 'em a cup of coffee. Did you get the coffeecake yesterday like I told you?"

"Yes," Josie called out, as Margaret hurried to the kitchen.

Josie opened the front door. Two elderly women smiled at her sadly.

"Hello, Josephine," said the first.

"My God," Josie said, "Mary McCaffrey—and Sarah."

"Hello, Josie," the second woman said. "We're sorry for your trouble."

"Thank you, Sarah. Come in."

"We was readin' the death notices in the *Trib* the other day," the first woman said, removing her gloves, "and I says,

'My God, Sarah,' I says, 'Bridget Scanlan passed away, God bless her.' So here we are."

"It's good of you to come," Josie said, closing the door. The two proceeded to the casket, taking out handkerchiefs.

"Ah, she looks beautiful," Mary said.

"Ah, God bless her," Sarah said. "I haven't seen the poor soul in—it must be two, three years. I kept saying, I said, 'Mary, we ought to go visit the Scanlans and see how poor Bridget is but—you know how it is, Josie—Mary ain't been too well herself and my brother Pat fell off a boxcar down at the yards and broke his back—"

"Oh, that's too bad," Josie said.

Both women knelt to pray. After a moment the front door opened again and Mike Scanlan entered.

"Oh," Josie said, "it's you."

"Yeah," Mike whispered sarcastically. "Who were you expectin'—the Pope?"

"Ssshh!" Josie said, "Mary and Sarah McCaffrey are here. Couldn't you get decently dressed, even today?"

Without answering, Mike hung up his cap and overcoat in a closet in the vestibule.

"Come here," Josie said, attempting to smell his breath.

"Not a drop," he said, annoyed. "Is Davey up?"

"He's out playing. It doesn't seem right to me, but Maggie seemed to think that—"

Mike dismissed her with a wave, then crossed and looked into the coffin. After a moment he removed from his back pocket a large railroad man's dark blue handkerchief with small white dots. Quickly he dabbed his eyes and blew his nose. Mary McCaffrey rose from the knee rest.

"Oh, hello, Mike," she said.

"Hello, Mary."

"How are ya?"

"Just fine," Mike said, smiling faintly. "How's yourself?"

"Fine, thanks. It's a great shame, Mike, your poor mother passin' on."

"Yes, I guess so," he said. "I mean—that's right."

"Mike, how are ya?" Sarah said, rising stiffly to her feet.

"Pretty good, Sarah," Mike said. "It's nice to see ya. How's Pat, by the way?"

"Oh, I was just telling Josephine, the poor soul had a terrible fall down at the yards."

"I'm sorry to hear that."

"Yes, a terrible fall. Broke his back."

Mike shook his head in sympathetic dismay.

"Are ya still workin' for the Northwestern yourself?" Sarah said.

"Uh—no," he said. "I—I quit down there quite some time ago. I—I've been out of town for some time."

"Yes," Josie said, quickly. "Mike's been at the Soldiers' Home in Danville. Listen, can I get you two a cup of tea?"

"No, thank you, Josie," Mary said. "We'll just sit here and relax ourselves. Don't you worry about us now. You just go on about your business, you and Mike. There'll be others comin' in that we can talk to."

"That's right," Sarah said. "We'll be fine right here."

The two visitors seated themselves in the parlor and began silently to finger rosary beads.

"I'll be right back," Josie said, as she returned to her bedroom.

Mike walked to the kitchen, whistling an old song. As he entered, Tommy Monaghan and John O'Toole rose from the table to greet him.

"Oh, hello, Tom, Jack," Mike said. "How are ya?"

"How's yourself, Mike?" Tommy asked.

"We're sorry to hear about your poor mother," O'Toole said.

"Thanks," Mike said. "Well, the poor old soul was eighty-six, ya know."

"Yeah, the poor old soul," O'Toole muttered. A silence fell over the room.

"Maggie just put hot water on for a cuppa coffee," Tom said, "but I . . . uh . . . I ain't much in the mood for *coffee,* are you, Jack?"

"Jeez, no," O'Toole said, firmly.

"Me neither," Tommy added.

"Me neither," Mike agreed. "Say, if either o' you fellas is holdin' today I could run down to Slattery's place and bring back a can o' suds."

"Fine idea!" O'Toole said, looking through his pockets. "I got . . . uh . . . fifty-seven cents on me, but I got to save fourteen o' that for car fare."

"I'm kinda short myself," Tom confessed. "Let's see . . . I can't spare more than two bits."

"I got four bits of my own," Mike said, as he took their

17

small change. "We'll put it all together and that should take care of us for a while."

"Don't get none o' that *near* beer now," O'Toole said. "Jeez, there's a Polack landlady in our buildin' and I swear to Christ she's tryin' to poison us all with her Goddamned *near* beer."

"Not near enough, huh?" Tom said, laughing.

"You said it," O'Toole said grimly. "Boy, a Depression and Prohibition are one hell of a combination."

"You fellas make yourselves at home here," Mike said. "There's some sliced ham or baloney or somethin' in the ice-box if you want to make yourselves a sandwich. I'll be right back."

He drew a gray metal pail from the cupboard and walked out the back screen door.

"Say, Tom," O'Toole said, after a moment, "were you holdin' out on Mike? You worked three days this week."

"Sure, I got a few bucks in my kick, and they're gonna stay there. I ain't gonna spend my last cent buyin' beer for Mike Scanlan, God knows."

"Right," O'Toole said. "You're absolutely right."

"Sure, it's *his* mother's dead in there, not mine," Tom said, "God rest her soul."

"Right," O'Toole said. "I don't mind chippin' in a few cents but I'll be damned if it's up to you and me to keep big Mike in beer." He paused. "And sure, it'd take the national debt to do that, anyway."

"It certainly would," Tom agreed. "I hope we didn't do the

wrong thing givin' him anything at all. He's been on the wagon lately, ya know."

"Yes, I know. And I for one wish he'd stay on it. God, he can be a mean drunk if you cross him." O'Toole laughed. "Tom, do ya remember the time years ago when the Rafferty brothers tried to throw him outta their place on 47th and Halsted, and after they did, sure he picked up the two o' them and threw *them* back *in!*"

"Yeah." Tom laughed. "He's mean sometimes when he's drinkin'. It's a shame, too. When he was young, why there wasn't anybody in this part o' Chicago who could stand up to him. Even the coppers wouldn't tackle him unless there was three of 'em. But now he's over the hill and he don't know it, so the poor bastard keeps gettin' into fights with younger fellas."

"And some o' them give him an awful beatin'," O'Toole said, frowning.

"Just awful."

"Ah, God," O'Toole sighed sadly. "*All* the good men in this neighborhood are over the hill. These young characters around here today, I don't understand 'em at all. They'd as soon kill ya as look at ya."

Mike hurried along Cottage Grove Avenue toward 47th Street, whistling. Then, feeling guilty about sounding so carefree with his mother newly dead, he stopped. In the doorway of an out-of-business cleaning shop he saw the body of a derelict and stepped past the man without looking back. Booze and the Depression had littered Chicago with the unconscious forms of broken men, most of them inhabiting the Madison Street and Clark Street neighborhood on the near North Side Skid Row, but others to be found here and there all over the city. They could be seen alone or in groups, huddled in alleys, sharing a bottle, killing themselves with raw alcohol or the squeezings of canned heat, all thin, red-faced, poorly dressed, half dead from the heat of summer or the crushing cold of winter.

Incapable of work and unable to find it when they tried, they lived either by putting the touch on passersby or taking fives and tens from the saddened women of their families—sisters, mothers, more rarely wives. Some, veterans, got a little government pension money. Mike, who had himself upon occasion been reduced to raising carfare or the money for a drink by putting the bite on better dressed men or women on the street, was nevertheless not one of the totally, irrevocably lost homeless alcoholics. But he had done more than one tour of duty among them. He was no stranger to the desperate, haunting compulsion that made the next drink seem literally the most important thing in the world, no stranger to the warm, easy glow from the first drink, the desperate lunge for an even higher plateau of relaxation and comfort, never attained, but always replaced by a fuzzy-minded truculence or rising irritability, an angry courage that led him to make abusive threats. Sometimes his aggressiveness went unchallenged but other times he would be answered, perhaps by another drunk, perhaps by a sober stranger. There were fights, which in earlier years he had won but which now ended as often in defeat and pain.

He would stay away from home at such times, at least for a few days, sleeping in Madison Street flophouses if he could raise the price. He'd spent lost, painful nights in dozens of them across the country. They were all the same: long flights of narrow stairs in ancient, run-down buildings, dim hallways and rows of rude army-type cots in large, bare rooms. For an extra dime or quarter you could have a special "room," which meant that your bed was surrounded by chicken wire. The wire fencing afforded no privacy. It merely discouraged theft of your shoes or jacket. It wasn't a bad idea to roll up all your clothes and put them under your pillow, assuming you took them off at all. Otherwise, some wino desperate for a drink and without the price would steal anything he could get his hands on, hoping to sell it for a nickel or a dime.

At Slattery's Restaurant, the back room of which was considered a "speakeasy," Mike put such thoughts out of his mind and ordered his bucket of beer, which he then carried home partially covered by a sheet of newspaper although no policeman on the South Side would have given the bucket a second glance if it had been a barrel. Nor, for that matter, was there an officer within ten miles of Slattery's place who didn't know what was going on there. Prohibition was something that only Protestants and certain federal police cared a damn about. To all others it was a farce and a nuisance.

In the kitchen Margaret smiled at Monaghan.

"I guess that coffee must be hot by now, Tom," she said. "Yes, it is. It's not exactly fresh. We made it last night but I just wanted to hot it up a little for ya."

She set out two cups and saucers and poured both men steaming cups of coffee.

"Oh, don't trouble yourself, Mag," Tom said, nodding gratefully.

"No, we're perfectly all right, Mag," O'Toole said. "We had breakfast not an hour ago."

"I know," Margaret insisted. "But it's gettin' a little chilly out and a good hot cup of coffee'll warm yez up. I got some good coffeecake at Hillman's downtown yesterday."

She loved shopping at Hillman's, the enormous delicatessen, specialty and meat market downtown. There was something about the cool air of the place that she found refreshing. It always seemed at least a few degrees colder than the outside air, except in winter, and it was laden with the delicious mingled odors of salted meats, dill pickle barrels, mounds of sauerkraut, dried or fresh fish. Behind the meat counters shone scores of hung rabbits, chickens, turkeys, hams and sides and legs of beef or veal or lamb. Shaved ice and greens were everywhere, trimming and framing and preserving the meats and poultry. The store had marvelous baked goods on display—handsome cakes, tempting golden sweet rolls, rich chocolate éclairs and specialties from the many cultures that made up what was called the melting pot of Chicago but in which in reality very little melting took place. For the most part the different peoples—the Irish, the Germans, the Poles, Swedes, Italians, Jews, Greeks—kept to themselves, in their own neighborhoods, speaking their own languages or their own broken English, eating their own foods, hearing their own music, going to their own places of worship.

The Wake

Hillman's always seemed to Margaret somehow European although she had never traveled outside of the United States. She loved the German sauerkraut and fat, spicy wieners, the Jewish dill pickles, the Swedish breads and pastries, the Italian sausages from among which she would select with great care and bring home in thin cardboard cartons, wrapped with string, carrying them for hours on the streetcars home, to please the rest of the family.

For her two guests now she set out the flat cardboard container of coffeecake, glazed with white sugar cream and studded with brown nuts, and set a piece for each man.

"Thanks, Mag," Tom said. "It does look like good coffee-cake at that."

"Just when did your mother pass away, Mag?" O'Toole said, crossing his legs.

"In her sleep, God help her, last . . . let's see. Yes, two nights ago. She hadn't been well for quite some time and I suppose we all knew she was dyin'. But I don't think *she* did."

"She was the sweetest old soul I ever knew, God bless her," O'Toole said.

"That's right, John," Tom added. "That she was. That she was indeed."

"And to think, Mag, that she outlived most of her children."

"Yes, isn't that odd now?" Margaret said. "I was just sayin' to Josie last night, I said, 'Just think, Josie, Joe is dead, Pat is dead, Annie is dead. All of 'em in their graves at least thirty years before Ma.' And then, of course, there were the

23

ones that died as children, most of 'em before the rest of us came along."

"The poor old soul gave birth to how many of yez in all, Mag? Eleven, isn't it?" Tom said.

"Twelve," Margaret said. "Six of them died before they reached the age of five, and then there were the rest of us."

"Joe was the oldest of you, wasn't he?" O'Toole asked.

"Of *our* group, yes," Margaret said. "Let's see. There was Joe, then Annie, then Pat, then Josie, then Belle, then Rose . . ."

"I always liked Rose," O'Toole said, with a broad smile.

"She always liked you too, John," Margaret recalled. "Anyway, after Rose came Jack, then big Mike, the baby . . ." she chuckled. "Some baby he turned out to be. Where is he, by the way?"

"Oh," Tom said, "he stepped out for a minute. To pick up some . . . uh . . . Bull Durham tobacco, I think he said it was."

"He'll be right back, he said," O'Toole added. "Where *is* Rose, incidentally?"

"Oh, God," Margaret said. "I'm heartsick from wonderin'. Neither she nor Belle have gotten here yet. I sent 'em both telegrams. I know that Belle got hers 'cause I talked to her on the phone. But you know how Rose is about telephones. She won't answer 'em unless she's in the mood, so I don't even know if she heard about Ma dyin' yet."

"Wouldn't she read about it in the paper?" O'Toole said.

"Well, Tommy," Margaret said, "it wasn't exactly on the front page of the *Trib*, ya know. If she looked at the death notices the last few days she'll know. But, otherwise, maybe not. I don't even know if she got my wire. I suppose if we don't hear from her tomorrow I'll have to go over to her place myself, but I ain't in the mood for a ride all the way over to the North Side, I'll tell ya that."

"What's Mike been doin' with himself lately?" Tom said.

"He hasn't been able to find work ever since he was laid off down at the freight yards. Although I don't know how hard he's been lookin'. He was at the Veterans' Hospital in West Allis, Wisconsin, for a while. Or was it Danville? Well, anyway . . . then he came back. It's a good thing he did, too. I think Ma died happy just knowin' that he was here at home. She always worried herself sick about him when he was away."

"Well," O'Toole said, "him bein' the youngest and all."

"I guess she figured the rest of us could take care of ourselves. But himself she was always worried about. And another good thing—he was on the wagon, thank God, when she died. That's another reason I think she died happy."

David walked in, pink-cheeked from the cold.

"Hi, Aunt Mag," he said. "Is there any coffeecake left?"

"Sure, honey," she said. "My, you've got a big appetite today. Here, sit down and I'll give you some coffeecake and a glass of milk. What did you have for breakfast? Oh, yes, oatmeal. I can't seem to remember anything today."

She quickly sliced coffeecake, took a bottle of milk from the icebox, poured a glass for the boy and set it on the table.

"You know Mr. O'Toole and Tommy Monaghan," she said.

"Sure, Davey," Tom said. "How are you?"

"Fine, thanks."

"He's a handsome boy, Mag," O'Toole said. "Looks a lot like his late father, I understand."

"Yes," Margaret said. "Oh, Davey, the icebox pan has leaked all over the floor. Will you empty it, honey?"

"Sure." Kneeling, David carefully drew the wide, gray pan full of water from under the icebox and poured it into the sink.

He rarely saw the iceman, a giant Swede, who wore a black leather vest and carried enormous blocks of dripping ice, lifting them with his dark iron tongs, to all the apartments in the neighborhood. His deliveries were usually made during the hours when David was in school, but during the long, hot summers then the iceman on his rounds was a frequently seen and always welcome figure. At the sight of his old lumbering truck, with its solid-rubber wheels, the children would shout with glee and run forward from dingy alleys and dusty lots to stand and watch as the Iceman—whose name was never known—would park his juggernaut with a rusty squeal of brakes, swing down out of the driver's seat, walk back to the rear of the truck, step up on the battered wooden back platform and, from the cool cavern that was the truck's interior, withdraw a large gleaming, dripping block of crystal, flecked with bits of sawdust.

When he had hoisted it to a meaty shoulder, scowled at the children in warning, and disappeared around the corner of a nearby building, David and his friends would descend on the truck like locusts, sticking their heads into the ice compartment, sniffing the cool air, inhaling the odor of the hot canvas top and that of the wet wooden floor. Always there would be a few scraps and chips of ice lying about. Sweaty hands would clutch them and put them into greedy, thirsty mouths. If you got a chunk large enough you could rub it over your hot face and along the back of your neck. If the piece was too large to fit into your mouth you cracked it on the sidewalk or a brick wall to reduce it to fragments of manageable size.

Sometimes, if a girl was present, one of the boys might drop a small piece of ice down the collar of her dress, in back of course, since to have dropped it down the front would have been an unthinkable crime. Or one of the boys might finger a glistening nugget till his hand was dripping with water then flick it at a friend, spotting his shirt with quick black drops that promptly disappeared in the blazing heat of the summer sun.

Then perhaps there would be another foray up and half-way into the dim, refreshing cave, broken by shouts of warning that the Iceman was coming back. "Jiggers! Here he comes!" And off they would fly, squealing, like a flock of startled birds, back to their innocent games and adventures.

Margaret took the cardboard ice sign from the sideboard.
"I forgot to put the iceman's sign up last night," she said. "He should have delivered twenty-five pounds this morning. Well, I guess this little piece'll get us by till tomorrow." She walked to the window and propped the sign up, face out,

against the frame. O'Toole rose to look somewhat uneasily out the window.

"Uh, Tom," he said. "Your eyes are better than mine. Can you see if that fella comin' down the street is Mike or not?"

Tom moved to the window. "I can't quite make out, John," he said. "Whadda ya say we step out here on the back porch and get a breath of fresh air ourselves?"

"Fine," O'Toole said quickly. "We'll just be out here for a minute, Mag. You go on about your business now. Don't let us detain you."

"That's all right. Just make yourselves at home." The two men, having finished their coffeecake and coffee, stepped outside to intercept Mike.

"Exactly when is Mama Belle coming home, Aunt Mag?" David said.

"I think she'll be here some time today, honey," Margaret said, as she began to tidy up the dishes left on the table.

"Are you sure?"

"*Pretty* sure. She sent a wire day before yesterday that I think meant she'd be here this morning."

"But it's almost afternoon."

"Well, the trains are probably late. Don't worry, honey. She'll be here."

"Boy, I sure hope so." David toyed with the red and green pattern of the oilcloth on the table. "How long has it been since I've seen her, Aunt Mag?"

"I don't know, sweetheart. A few weeks, I think."

"Seems more like months to me."

"Well, weeks add up to months."

"They sure do," the boy said, chin in hand. "Why can't she work here in Chicago?"

"Well, there's only a few theatres in this town where they have vaudeville. Even if she played all of 'em she'd eventually have to go on the road. You know that."

"Yeah." He paused and sighed. "I wish I didn't have to go to school."

"Now isn't that a silly thing to say. Don't you want to get smart and grow up to be a civil engineer or somebody important like that?"

"Oh, I don't know."

"You don't want to go to school because you'd rather be livin' with your Mama Belle than with me, is that it?"

"Well, I guess so," David said. "We used to have a lot of fun when I was with her all the time. You know what I used to love? Staying at the Hotel Sherman downtown in the Loop and eatin' breakfast in bed and havin' the waiter bring the food in on a great big tray with a big silver coffeepot on it that was full of nice hot cocoa. Boy, I used to have all the cocoa I wanted. Five or six cups if I wanted."

"Well, honey, you can have all the cocoa you want here, too."

"I know, but it isn't as much fun here. I mean we don't have a big silver pot that holds five or six cups, and besides when I look out the window here there's nothin' to see but the street. But when I looked out the window at the Hotel Sherman I could see the whole city, practically."

"Well, that's just because you was way up on a high floor.

Don't worry, honey. Mama Belle will be here some time today. You'll see."

Later in the morning David decided to take another close look at his grandmother although he felt frightened about doing so. The first time he had felt vaguely uneasy but he had had to kneel and say a prayer, conscious that the others in the room were looking at him, so that the experience passed quickly. It had seemed unreal. Now that he was wider awake and no one was telling him what to do he thought perhaps he would go up close to the coffin and look at the old lady again.

As he approached the body he looked first at the flames of the candles, then at the brightly colored flowers that almost filled the wall against which the coffin was placed. Then at last he was standing next to the body and looking down at it. He felt alternately numb and slightly fearful. He had seen plenty of dead bodies in the movies. Dead cowboys, dead Indians, dead townspeople in *Frankenstein* and *Dracula* pictures, dead soldiers, dead gangsters. But he had never before seen an actual dead body himself. He remembered having seen his Grandma Considine shortly before she died, looking strange and speaking to him in an odd whispery way. He had not liked the smell in the bedroom and could not now remember anything else about that particular death. But now, looking down at the grandmother he had known so well, had seen daily for so long a time, he felt a strange mixture of emotions. Fear. Sadness. Confusion. Coldness.

The catechism said that his grandmother was already gone,

to heaven, he assumed. But then what was this left behind that looked exactly like her? Her body, of course. He did not understand, really, what a soul was and so it began to seem to him rather that the old woman was just peacefully asleep. Once, standing there, he almost thought he saw something in her face move.

CHAPTER TWO

In the next moment they heard the sound of heavy, frantic banging at the front door.

"Glory be to God," Margaret said, "who could that be? You wait here, honey. I'll see who it is."

She ran from the kitchen along the hallway, meeting Josie, who entered from one of the bedrooms.

"Who *is* that at the door?" Josie said. Again came a loud knocking.

"It must be either Rose or Belle. Now, Josie, don't start a fight."

"Me? Why in the name of God would *I* start a fight? I'm not one of the hell raisers in this family. If there's trouble this morning in the sight of poor Ma's coffin you mark my words, Maggie, it'll be Rosie or Belle that'll start it."

"Oh, be quiet, for God's sake, Josie, while I see who it is." When she opened the door her sister Rose rushed in, wild-eyed.

"Where is she, Maggie?" she cried.

"Rose, be quiet," Margaret said. "There are people in there."

"Get out of my way!" Rose shouted. Rushing to the coffin

she threw herself, crying brokenly, across her mother's body.

"Oh, Ma, Ma, Ma! Oh, God. Ma. What have they done to you?"

"Rosie, please," Margaret said.

"Ma, God love you, Ma!" Rose said. "Maggie, why didn't you tell me she was sick?"

"Rose, you *knew* she was sick."

"Certainly I knew it. Didn't I make good hot stew and bring it to this house myself only two weeks ago. But I didn't know she was—" She broke into lamentation again. "Oh, God, Ma, Ma! God love you. I love you, Ma. I love you."

"Rose," Josie said, coldly, "Mary and Sarah McCaffrey are here."

"Oh, that's all right, Josie," Mary said. "We understand."

"Certainly," Sarah said. "Hello, Rose."

Rose collapsed on her knees and crossed herself. "In the Name of the Father, and of the Son and of the—*ahhhhh!*" She wept uncontrollably again.

"Rose," Josie said, "try to pull yourself together. We all feel the same way about poor Ma."

"You shut up, you bitch," Rose flung at her.

"Josie," Margaret said, "I told you to keep your mouth shut."

"I'd a-been living with poor Ma to her dyin' day," Rose said, facing Josie, "if it wasn't for you, you bulldozer! The only reason I married Charlie O'Brian in the first place was to get away from you and the boys and your constant nagging and bullying. Who the hell do you think you *are* to keep me away from Ma?"

33

"Don't be blamin' me for your own foolishness, Rosie," Josephine said, forgetting the McCaffrey sisters. At that moment David ran in from the kitchen, calling, "Aunt Mag."

"Rose, will you shut up and sit down!" Margaret said. "What must poor Ma think if she can see us all here, fighting over her poor dead body, God rest her soul."

Rose fell into a chair and wept.

"What's the matter, Aunt Rosie?" David said, feeling afraid in his stomach.

"Never mind, Davey," Margaret said soothingly. "Aunt Rose isn't feeling well. You run along now, into another room, or go outside and play some more and leave us alone."

"All right." The boy picked up his sweater and went out to the street.

"Maybe we'd better be leavin', Mag," Mary said.

"Yes," Sarah added, "I think we'd better."

"Oh, that's all right, Sarah," Margaret said. "I guess the worst is over now. You see, poor Rose didn't know that Ma was dead until today, I guess. The shock was too much for her."

"Rosie, have you been drinking?" Josie said.

"You're Goddamned right I have, and what the hell business is it of yours! I had one lousy glass of beer to steady my nerves on the way over here, as God is my judge, and I don't have to take any abuse from *you* about it!"

"Josie," Margaret said, "will you leave her alone."

"Oh, it's my fault, is it?" Josie said, beginning to pace like an angry animal. "Well, I've had about as much of this as I

34

can take! I moved to California just to get away from all this and I'm going back there just as soon as I can, believe me."

"Who's keepin' ya?" Rose shouted. "Go, go, you fat slob!"

"Maggie, you'd better tell her to keep a civil tongue in her head or she'll be sorry. I know a few things about that one that Charlie O'Brian would be mighty interested in hearing." Josie stomped to her bedroom and slammed the door. Rose fell to her knees and began to pray again, beside the coffin. "Oh, God, forgive me. Bless me, Father, for I have sinned." She blew her nose loudly and began to pray, under her breath. "Hail, Mary, full of grace—"

"You sure you wouldn't rather be alone, Marge?" Sarah McCaffrey said.

"No, Sarah, that's all right. You know us well enough, for God's sake. You know what the problem is."

"Listen," Mary said, "it's the same in all families, God forgive us. Sure, just last Saturday, on the way home from confession, my brother Matty got frightened by the mean chow dog that belongs to that Wop gardener that lives over on Green Street and sure, he was after gettin' absolution and feelin' so good and all, why, he and the Wop said such terrible things to one another Matty couldn't even go to Communion the next morning. And he stayed mad for the rest of the week. By the way, speakin' of my brother—is your brother Jack comin' to the wake?"

"I don't know, Sarah," Margaret said, "I sent a wire to the paper he works for in Boston but since we ain't heard from him in almost a year I'm not even sure if he's there any more. Oh, he sent Ma a postcard from Paris, France, when he was there about six months ago doin' somethin' or other for the paper, but I don't know. I just don't know."

"Well, God is good," Sarah said. "Whoever got the wire may forward it to him if he doesn't work there any more."

"I certainly hope so," Margaret said tiredly. "This family is scattered to the four winds. Sometimes I miss the days when we was all together. And yet you can see what happens when we're all under the same roof."

David had been shocked by his Aunt Rose's emotional outburst. Her nose had been running and she had been slightly unsteady on her feet. He never liked to see any member of the family in such a condition, though he often had, and if strangers were present there was added a hideous embarrassment to his shock and dismay.

Though he did not see Rose often and her husband, Charlie, less, he liked the two of them simply because they were gentle and affectionate to him. Rose, who was thin, and Charlie, who was fat, had no children of their own and lavished all their affection on their dog, a brown and white mongrel named Puppo. On the infrequent occasions when David would visit them, or they would come to visit the family, they smiled at David and patted him in much the same way that they smiled at and patted their dog.

The oddest thing about them was that they would sometimes communicate by talking to the dog instead of addressing each other directly. Instead of saying, "Charlie, are you ready for your dinner?" Rose would say, talking in a strange kind of baby talk, "Puppo, you ask Charlie O'Brian, you ask your daddy, if he is ready for his dinnuh. That's right. That's what you do, Puppo. Go on. You trot right over there and ask your daddy if he wants his dinnuh."

Charlie would say, also in baby-talk accents, "Puppo, you tell Mama you and me, we been waitin' for our dinnuh for a long, *long* time. Yes, sir. Yessiree, sir. You just go right up to her and you say, 'Mama, I want my dinnuh.' That's right. '*I want my dinnuh.*'"

At such times they would look at the dog as they spoke, scratch his ears and rub his back, but the messages were mainly for each other. Sometimes they would even discuss things that would have been of no earthly interest to the dog even if he had been able to understand English.

"Puppo-boy," Charlie might say, "you tell you' mama that Charlie, he goin' down to the drugstoah, and he goin' get some Alka-Seltzuh. You heah me? You heah me, Puppo? You tell you' mama that Charlie be right back. He goin' down to the old drugstoah on the cornuh. That's right. That's where he goin'."

And Rose would say something like "Puppo, you tell Charlie O'Brian that Mama and Puppo, they gonna look out the window and watch him go down the street. That's right. They gonna stand right up here by the window, and look out and look *aaallllll* around. And they gonna say, 'Daddy, you bettuh hurry right back.' Yes, sir. 'You bettuh hurry right back heah or we gonna *worry* about you.' Puppo, he gonna say, 'Daddy, where'd you go?' And he gonna *howl* at the window and the landlady she gonna bang on the door and oh my goodness, it gonna be *awful*."

They would sometimes talk to each other like that at great

length. It usually made David feel embarrassed but on the other hand it seemed a little funny, too. At least it was better than Aunt Rose coming in smelling of drink and staggering around and acting all loud and crazy.

Another odd thing about Uncle Charlie was that because he was fat he liked to talk about food. Or was it the other way around? Anyway, he would tell you about a good dinner he had had in the way other men might tell you about some accident or adventure they had been involved in. "And, by golly, I musta had three helpin's of mashed potatoes and gravy. Rose, nobody can make chicken gravy like you can. And wasn't that a great lemon cream pie I brought home?"

Good cook though she was, Rose apparently did not bake pies, so Charlie was forever going to this or that bakery about the city shopping for pies. Apple, peach, chocolate cream, blueberry. His favorite was lemon cream, very thick with the white top singed brown in the oven and the yellow filling not too soft and not too dry. Whenever David ate at their apartment he would be given a large wedge of lemon-cream pie for dessert and Charlie might say, "Isn't that great, Davey? Isn't that the greatest lemon-cream pie you ever ate? I got it over in Jew-town. Would you like more? Go ahead, I got another one in the icebox. And you can have all you want. Got to put some meat on those bones of yours."

No matter how much he ate David never seemed to gain any more weight than his natural growth dictated. But he liked Charlie for his generosity, his good humor and his gentleness.

His Aunt Rose could be mean, like all the women in the

family except Aunt Mag, but Charlie seemed to put up with her abuse without complaining much. Except once. Only one time had David seen his uncle angry and that once was enough to frighten him so badly he never forgot the incident. He had come to visit the two of them, two years earlier when they had lived in the same neighborhood, walking over to their apartment himself, and when he got to the door of their apartment Charlie looked down, red-faced, and said, "Oh, hi there, old-timer. Say, Aunt Rose isn't feelin' too well right now. Whadda ya say you and me go down to the Greek restaurant on the corner? I was just gonna have a bite of lunch."

So they went to the restaurant and sat at the marble counter. David looked at the menu in a folder covered with plastic, and decided he would have a bowl of vegetable soup and a ham sandwich. His uncle ordered a hot roast beef sandwich with potatoes and gravy. While they waited for the food, making small talk, David noticed that his uncle was breathing heavily, in an odd way. Suddenly David saw his Aunt Rose move past the plate-glass window and to the door of the restaurant, her hair mussed up.

She flung the door wide and stood there with a sneer on her face. "Oh," she said. "So this is where you're hidin' out!" At that his previously gentle, good-natured uncle jumped to his feet, shouted, "Goddamn you!" in a hoarse voice, picked up a heavy glass tumbler and hurled it, as fast as a baseball, at Rose. The projectile missed her, crashing through the glass top of the open door behind her. She turned and ran. The

Greek manager hurried out of the kitchen and said, "Wait a minute here! Wait a minute. What's happening?"

Charlie stood with his fists clenched, staring at the door, then slowly turned to the man behind the counter.

"I'm sorry," he said. "I'll pay all the damages. I just lost my temper."

David was too frightened to speak. He sat at the counter staring down at the menu, in embarrassment, feeling numb and blank between waves of fear, while his uncle began to help the manager clean up the broken glass.

In the kitchen, Tommy and O'Toole welcomed Mike and his pail of foaming beer.

"The coast is clear," he said. "Come on." He took three glasses—actually old jelly jars—from the cupboard and poured out three cold beers.

"Here's how," he said. They all drank with gusto.

"Jeez," Mike said, "I wish Jack was here to have a glass of beer with us."

"Ain't he comin'?" O'Toole asked.

"I don't know. Mag wired him, but we haven't heard anything back. He'll be sick if he hears later that he missed Ma's funeral." He paused, staring into his glass. "I always thought he was her favorite."

"Where is Jack now," Tom said, "still overseas?"

"I don't think so," Mike said. "I think he's workin' for a paper in Boston again."

"Somebody was tellin' me poor Jack left the Church, Mike," O'Toole said, quietly.

"I don't know. Maybe he did. But he didn't leave the human race. If he got that wire, he'll be here. It'll be good to see him."

"Yes, it will," Tom said smiling. "He's quite a guy. Say, Mike, do you remember when Jack was at the seminary years ago—" He turned to O'Toole. "He was studyin' for the priesthood, ya know, John."

"Yes," O'Toole said. "So I understand."

"Anyway, I didn't see this myself, but I heard tell that one night he got into the cathedral or whatever the hell it was, and started playing the big pipe organ to beat the band. Only he was playin' "Alexander's Ragtime Band." They say him and three other fellows almost got kicked out of the seminary for that one." They all laughed.

Mike said, after a sigh, "Funny how life is."

"Yeah," O'Toole said, "ain't it though?"

"Say," Tommy said, lighting a cigarette, "I didn't realize that the kid was livin' with all of you again."

"Oh, yeah," Mike said, "and I'm glad he is. He's a good boy. Belle can't keep him with her on the road, I guess. She tried to now and then when he was just a little shaver, but once he got big enough to go to school it was no dice. She had him in a boarding school out west for a while, but Christ, that must be like doin' time at Joliet."

"And you ought to know what that's like, eh, Mike?" O'Toole said.

They all laughed again.

"To hell with you," Mike said. "Anyway, he spends some of his time with the Considines, his father's family, and some of the time with Mag here, and some of the time with his mother. But not much. It's a damned shame his father died. When I'm around I see quite a bit of him, but I ain't much of a father, I guess."

"Mike," Tom said, "it's too bad you never got married. You might have made a hell of a father."

"Aw, go on. I got better things to do than that."

The doorbell sounded softly.

Josie, coming out of her room, said, "Maggie, is that the—"

"Never mind, Josie. I'll get it," Margaret said.

When she opened the door there stood a small, middle-aged, somewhat seedy-looking man with a Roman collar. Margaret did not recognize him.

"Hello," he said, "I'm Father Morrisey."

"Oh, hello, Father. Come in. Forgive me, I didn't remember you. I mean, I wasn't expecting you."

"That's all right. I just happened to be in the neighborhood and I thought I'd come in for a few minutes and pay my respects. Mrs. Scanlan was a fine woman. It was a great shock to hear of her passing."

"Can I take your coat, Father?"

"No, thanks. I can't stay long. But I did want to just drop in, as I say, and tell you how sorry I am."

Mike entered, saying, "Say, Maggie, how in the name of God are we going to—" He stopped as he saw the priest. "Oh, pardon me, Father."

Margaret turned to him. "Mike, this is Father . . . uh, Morrisey, did you say, Father?"

"Yes, that's right. Father Morrisey. You're Mike Scanlan, are you?"

"Yes, Father."

"Well, I was just telling your wife that I was the—"

"My *wife?*" Mike frowned.

"I'm Margaret Scanlan, Father. I'm Mike's *sister*." As Rose came into the vestibule Margaret said, "This is my sister Rose."

"Ah, I see," the visitor said. "Good morning. Excuse me just a minute." He stepped to the coffin, knelt, made the sign of the Cross and prayed briefly.

David came in, whistling absent-mindedly. "Who's that, Aunt Maggie?"

"Sshh, Davey. That's Father Morrisey from St. Ambrose."

"I don't know him," David whispered.

"Well, never mind. Don't make any noise." Mike noticed something in the hall, walked to the vestibule and returned after a moment with a floral piece in a white wicker basket. He placed the display with other flowers near the coffin.

"Who's that one from?" Margaret said.

"The Swede on the corner," Mike said.

"Who?"

"Olson, the bakery man on the corner."

"Well, now wasn't that nice of him?" Margaret said. "And I don't think Ma'd been in there for months. Well, listen, we give him a lot of business." The visitor rose to his feet.

"Well, Miss Scanlan," he said, "I won't be taking much of your time. But I did want to stop by for just a minute and tell you how really sorry I was—how sorry *all* of us were—to hear of your mother's passing. She was a wonderful woman."

"Thank you, Father," Rose said, on behalf of them all.

"It'd be a pleasure for me," the visitor said, "to say some Masses for the repose of her dear soul."

"Well, that's very kind of you, Father," Margaret said. "Are you new at St. Ambrose?"

"What?"

"I don't believe we've met before."

"Uh, no. That is, I'm not connected with St. Ambrose."

"See, I told you, Aunt Mag," David said.

"No," said the little man, "I'm down at St. Rita's."

"Oh, really?" Rose said.

"Yes. We didn't see your mother there very often. From time to time the poor soul would come to one of the early Masses there. That's how I got to know her."

"What?" Mike said, openly suspicious. "When was this?"

"Now, Mike," Margaret admonished, "take it easy."

"Well," said the little man, "I must be running along. By the way, if you'd care to have me say a few Masses for the repose of your poor mother's soul I'd be more than happy to, whether you feel like making a small donation or not. Believe me, it's not necessary. Although for the solemn High Mass next Sunday, of course, it probably wouldn't be a bad idea if—"

"Father," Mike said, with more of an edge to his voice, "I was just noticing: Your coat is a very dark *green* instead of the usual black."

"Now, Mike," Margaret said, "Father Morrisey might have made a mistake about Ma."

44

"A mistake?" said the visitor, moving slightly toward the door.

"Yes," Margaret said. "You see, Father, my mother hasn't been out of the house in two years, and as far as I know she never set foot in St. Rita's in her whole life."

"Oh," Morrisey said, "well, I—I can't understand that. Her name *is*—or *was*—Bridget Scanlan, isn't that right?"

"You're damn right it was, Father," Mike said. "But how do we know *your* name is Father Morrisey?"

"Now, Mike," Margaret said, "for God's sake don't cause trouble. You can't talk to a priest like that. I'm sorry, Father. He's had a couple of beers and, well, you know. Maybe you'd better be running along after all, Father."

"You didn't explain yet about the dark green coat instead of the black, Father," Rose said, rising and placing her fists on her hips.

"Just what the hell kind of a priest *are* you, anyway?" Mike said, raising his voice. The McCaffrey sisters sat like two old birds, taking it all in.

"Mike," Margaret said, "that's no way to talk to a priest."

"Well," said the stranger, "I'm certainly sorry to cause you any trouble. If you don't care to have me remember your mother in my Masses, I guess I'd better be running along."

"Oh, so *that's* it," Mike said. "You never met my mother in your life, but you thought you could come in here and raise a few bucks, huh?"

"Now, let me see," the little man said, "where did I leave my hat?"

"I'm sorry about this, Father," Margaret said, awkwardly.

"Don't listen to him. Davey, you run along and see if you can be of any help in the kitchen."

"I'm sorry for your trouble, Miss Scanlan," the man said, retrieving his hat. "If there's ever anything I can do for you—"

"Well, there's something you can do for *me* right now," Mike cut in, "and that's get the hell out of here."

"Mike, for God's sake," Rose said, "keep a civil tongue in your head when you're talking to a priest. What's come over you?"

"I'll tell you what's come over me. I don't think this bird is a priest at all."

"Then," said Margaret, "what do you keep calling him *Father* for?"

"Now see here . . ." the little man said, edging backward.

"Father, you son of a bitch," Mike said, "you get out of here before I break every bone in your body!" He advanced toward the stranger, who exited hastily, slamming the door behind him. Once he had achieved the safety of the sidewalk the impostor wiped his brow with a large handkerchief and said softly, "Holy Christ."

"Well," Margaret said, "that's a fine way to act in front of little Davey. Swearing at a priest, calling him a son of a bitch."

"I tell ya, I don't think he *was* a priest. I didn't like the look of his coat."

"Then what did you keep calling him *Father* for?"

"Well," Mike said, "I had to call him *something*."

"Oh, you sure did," Margaret said, "you had to call him a son of a bitch, that's what you called him all right."

"Yeah, Mike," Rose said, "maybe it wasn't right after all, callin' a priest a son of a bitch."

"Well, who called that son of a bitch a priest is what *I'd* like to know," Mike said.

"Can't you ever control your temper?" Margaret said.

"Ah, shut up."

"Don't raise your voice to me here in front of poor Ma," Margaret said.

"Oh, Jesus, Mary and Joseph, Maggie," Mike said, "the way you're talking you'd think she could hear us."

"Well, maybe she can."

"Well, if she can, then she can, but it doesn't have anything to do with whether or not we're standing here in front of her."

"Ah, shut up yourself," Margaret said, "you make me sick."

Sarah McCaffrey rose and came forward tentatively.

"Sure, and how could you tell for sure that he wasn't a real priest?" she said.

"By the cut of his *coat*," Mike said. "And the color. It was a dark green. Not black at all. You could see for yourselves."

"But," Sarah said, "maybe the poor soul was one o' them priests so poor himself that he couldn't afford a decent coat. You know, the kind that takes a vow of poverty."

"No," Rose said, "I don't think he was one o' them. And God knows, you don't have to take any *vows* about poverty these days. We've all got a touch of it, with or without the vows."

"Ain't it the truth," Mary McCaffrey said. David looked up at his aunt.

"Was he a bad man instead of a priest, Aunt Maggie?"

"We think so, honey. God forgive us if he wasn't. Well, I suppose we'll know for sure if we all get arrested."

"Or excommunicated," Rose said.

"Ah, I tell ya he was no good," Mike said. "I shoulda broke every bone in his body. Poor Ma lyin' there, and all this goin' on."

O'Toole and Tommy, having finished the beer, were drawn by the raised voices to the parlor.

"I think maybe we'd better be running along, Mag," Sarah said.

"Yes, I do, too," her sister said.

"Oh, that's all right, Sarah," Margaret said. "It's done now. You might as well just sit down."

"How've you been, Mary?" Rose asked.

"Just fine, Rose. And yourself?"

"Not too well. God, wouldn't you know they wouldn't leave us alone at a time like this."

"Hello, Rose," Tom Monaghan said warmly, shaking her hand. "What happened?"

"Hello, Tom," Rose said. "Ah, some phony bum pretended to be a priest so he could get in here and maybe steal somebody's purse."

"He tried to talk Maggie out of a ten spot," Mike said. "Or

maybe even more, pretendin' he was gonna say a Mass for Ma."

"He didn't," O'Toole said.

"I'm damned if he didn't. I'll bet he makes a good livin' just readin' the death notices and goin' to all the homes and wakes."

"Well," Rose said, "she had no rest while she was livin' so she can't be too surprised that it's all the same here now that she's dead."

"Ah, come on, fellas," Mike said. "Let's go back to the kitchen."

After the three men had gone down the hallway, Margaret said, "Sarah, Mary. Come on, sit down. Would you like a cup of tea?"

"I don't think so, Marge," Sarah said. "We'll just stay a little longer now." All the women seated themselves again in the parlor.

"Oh, if only I'd known, Maggie," Rose said. "If only I'd known how sick she was."

"I know, Rose," Margaret said, "but you won't answer your phone."

"Has Belle been here yet?" Rose said.

Margaret gave her a signal that David was listening. "No, not yet. She should be here today. We sent word to her in St. Louis."

While looking at the cards on the floral displays, David said, "Mama and Doug Roberts have been workin' the

Orpheum time. I write to her every week but sometimes I don't know where to send the letters."

"I know, honey," Rose said. "Well, she'll be here. You'll see."

Margaret rose and tried to read the cards on the flowers. "Davey, honey," she said, "would you go and find my glasses like a good boy. I think I left 'em in the bedroom somewhere."

"All right," David said. He walked slowly to the bedroom. When he was out of earshot Rose said, "Is she really coming?"

"God, I hope so," Margaret said. "Not so much for Ma's sake as for Davey's. His poor little heart'll be broke if she doesn't show up."

"And so will hers, I guess," Rose said. The McCaffrey sisters nodded in solemn unison.

"Ah, Mother of God," Margaret said, "why can't this family live in peace?"

"It's funny, Maggie," Rose said, blowing her nose. "That's just what Dada said to us all the night before he went away."

"Well, let's not be thinkin' about *that* now," Margaret said. "We've got enough trouble as it is without goin' back over twenty years lookin' for more, God knows."

"Do you ever hear from your father, Marge?" Sarah asked.

"No, Sarah. We don't. And we don't miss him, to tell the truth. Not any more, anyway. Twenty years o' time heals a lot of wounds. I suppose he was happier in the old country. It's more peaceful in County Cork than it is in this crazy city. He was never happy here."

David entered, carrying Margaret's glasses. "Here they are, Aunt Maggie. You left them on—"

At that moment the doorbell rang.

"I'll get it," he said, turning.

"No, wait," Rose said. "Don't answer it."

"Who do you suppose it is?" Margaret said. They had all begun to speak in whispers.

"Well, it might be anybody, Marge," Sarah said helpfully. "Just comin' to pay their respects."

"It's Mama Belle, I bet," David said. "Let me open the door, Aunt Mag."

"No, *wait*, David!" Rose said. "Mag, look out the window. See if you can see anybody. It might be the police. Maybe that was a real priest after all. That Mike'll have us all ruined yet with his temper."

"And there's nothin' wrong with your own," Margaret said, suddenly feeling trapped and irritable. She scurried to the window, drew back a shade and peered out.

"I don't see anybody," she said. The doorbell rang again and, after a moment, they heard impatient knocking.

"Would you like one of us to answer it, Rose?" Mary McCaffrey said. "That way if it's just a salesman or somebody you don't want to see we can tell 'em you're not available."

"Oh, yes," David said. "It might be Mama Belle. I bet it is. Please, hurry."

"All right," Margaret said, "I suppose this is silly. Open it, Sarah."

Sarah, who had moved closest to the door, now opened it slightly and looked out.

"Why, it's your brother Jack!" she said, stepping back.

Jack came in, wearing a fashionable topcoat and fedora,

forcing a smile through his impatience. "Well," he said, "is this the welcome I get?"

"Hi, Uncle Jack," David shouted.

"Hello, Davey-boy," Jack said, putting his hands on the boy's shoulders. "My goodness, but you're growing up tall. Oh, here's a little something I picked up for you." He handed the boy a bright blue yo-yo. "Hello, Maggie. Rose. What took you so long to answer the door?" His sisters half embraced him awkwardly.

"We thought it might be the police," Rose said.

"Things haven't changed a bit," Jack said, laughing heartily as he removed his coat and hat. "When did she die, Mag?"

"Three days ago," Margaret said. Her brother moved to the coffin and looked down at his mother. Slowly shaking his head, his eyes filling with tears, he said, "The poor old soul. I hope she didn't suffer."

"No, thank God," Margaret said. "It happened in her sleep, we think. I found her in the morning."

"Aren't you goin' to kneel down and say a prayer, Jack?" Rose said.

"Yes, I am, Rose," Jack said, edgily. "My heart's no different than your own."

He knelt quickly and stared again at his mother's face. Suddenly David, who had gone to the window, said, "Oh, boy!"

"What is it, Davey?" Margaret said. "What do you see?"

The boy turned away and looked crestfallen. "A yellow cab just turned into the street," he explained, "but it didn't stop."

CHAPTER THREE

Later in the morning David sat on the one flat stone step outside the apartment, straightening out the string of his new yo-yo, which had gotten twisted. Jack stood looking down at him.

"This is a keen yo-yo," David said.

"Oh, I would have got you something a little better, pardner," his uncle answered, "but I was in pretty much of a hurry to get here."

"That's okay."

"I guess you'll be mighty glad to see your mother again, eh?"

"Yeah," David said. "I think maybe this time she'll take me with her."

"Hey, that's great! Did your Aunt Mag say she would?"

"Not exactly," David said, "but now that Grandma's dead I don't see how I can stay here, do you? I mean, Aunt Maggie's at work all day so there'll be nobody here to take care of me."

"Ah," Jack said, "well now, ya know, I'm sure your mother'll *want* to have you with her again, but it might be a little tough to work it out." He studied the boy for a moment, then smiled.

"Listen," he said, "I've got an idea. If you wanted to come back to Boston with me for a while, why I'll bet we could have a *lot* of fun together. I could hire some sort of a maid to be around after you got out of school, and we could—"

"Well, thanks, Uncle Jack," David said, looking intently at his right thumbnail, "but I think I'd better go with Mama."

From inside the house his Aunt Margaret called, "Davey, are you out there?"

"Yes, Aunt Mag. I'm here with Uncle Jack."

"I just noticed you didn't make your bed, honey," Mag said. "Better do it now before you forget."

"Okay," David said.

For some time after David had gone into the building Jack stood looking about at what he could see of the great city he would always think of as home. The leaden sky and now blustery air echoed the lonely sensation that suddenly made him shudder. Rubbing his hands briskly together as if to reassure himself of his own material existence, he turned and entered the apartment. Josephine sat stonily in the parlor.

"Josie," he said in a whisper, "is there a drop in the house?"

"I think John O'Toole and Mike have some beer in the kitchen," she answered, frowning. "I hope nobody brings anything *stronger* into the house."

"Oh, don't worry," Jack said jauntily, "with poor Ma lyin' here I think you can trust us all."

"Well, you can handle it, but Mike can't. I hope you don't get him started."

"I think I'll just take a walk around the corner with some of the fellas and maybe pick up a little something," Jack said, making the decision in the instant, "in case somebody asks for it. We do have to be hospitable, ya know."

He walked to the kitchen where the men were still gathered.

"Come on, boys," he said. "Let's get a little fresh air. And I think we could all do with a drink, whadda ya say?"

"That's not a bad idea," O'Toole cried, jumping up.

They all followed Jack out the kitchen door.

Later David counted six more floral displays and baskets in the living room. There were now six people gathered around the coffin—his Aunt Josephine, the two McCaffrey sisters, a middle-aged woman he remembered only vaguely, Moll Fitzgerald, and two men in their fifties, Chuck McDermott and Mattie Mulcahey. Moll Fitzgerald knelt beside the coffin praying. After a moment she made the sign of the cross, rose and spoke to Josephine.

"She was a saint, Josie. An absolute saint. I'm sure she's in the sight o' God this minute."

"I keep thinkin' of all the things I could have done for her," Josie said.

"Oh, sure," Moll said. "That's the way it always is. When they're here it doesn't seem like they'll ever die so you think you've got a million years to make it all up to them. And then, all of a sudden, they're gone and it's too late to do anything."

"It's the strangest thing," Josie said. "I haven't even been able to cry yet. The right way, I mean. Oh, I've had a tear in my eye or a lump in my throat, but I—I don't know, I just feel numb. Maybe it's 'cause I can't really believe it."

"You ought to *let* yourself cry, Josie," Sarah McCaffrey said. "It'll do you good. I know what it is, believe me."

"Certainly," her sister agreed. "It'd do you a world of good."

"You find yourself thinking of the damndest things," Josie said. "Like tonight, Ma would've listened to 'Major Bowes'."

"That's right," Sarah recalled. "She loved that program. She'd never miss that—and she loved Maurice Seymour and the 'Irish Hour' on WCFL too."

"Yes, and 'Amos 'n' Andy'," Mary said.

David had always laughed, with Grandma, at Amos 'n' Andy, who he thought were actually Negroes. Andy was so dumb and he would always argue with Amos instead of listening to him, as he should have. David's favorite "Amos 'n' Andy" broadcast had been the one where Andy thought he was getting sick but he couldn't afford to go to the doctor so Amos said he would be glad to check out his throat just the way the doctors did. All they did was ask you to open your mouth and then they stuck a little piece of wood in and poked around and said, "Hmmm." So Amos did that for Andy but he didn't have a regular flat little piece of wood like the doctors used so he used the only piece of wood he had handy, which was a pencil. But the funny part was that it was an *indelible* pencil. So after a minute of poking and hmmming, Amos said, "Andy, you in worse trouble than I thought," and Andy said, "What you mean, Amos?" and Amos said, "Well,

I don't exactly know what you got but yo' mouth is full of
lots o' little purple spots."

David and his grandmother had laughed at that and they
had still laughed, months later, thinking back to the little
purple spots inside Andy's mouth. David loved to play with
indelible pencils, which Aunt Mag used in her work. She
would bring her papers home at night and sometimes sit in
an easy chair, or at the dining-room table, marking the bills
and papers, licking the point of the pencil and marking purple notations. David felt angry at the world when he considered what his aunt had to do to earn a living. She had to
walk many miles each day, around the "Loop"—which he
guessed just meant downtown Chicago—going to dozens of
offices where dishonest people worked who hadn't paid
money they owed to the Railway Express company.

She would tell stories about arguing with the people and
how they would lie to her and say things like "Well, now
I'm *sure* Mr. Levitt sent that money in last week," when Aunt
Mag knew they hadn't and that they were just being sneaky.
But she could always threaten them by saying that if they
didn't pay up pronto then the Railway Express company
wouldn't deliver their packages any more. That would usually make them pay up in a hurry. David didn't like these
people because, he thought, if they had just sent their money
in through the mail, the way they were supposed to, then
his old aunt could have had some easy job at an office instead
of having to trudge all over downtown, up and down thousands of stairs every day. She would come home utterly ex-
hausted, sometimes too tired to even take off her coat and hat

for quite a long time and would just sit down in a chair and stare straight ahead, or smile at David and give him some little present.

One program that David and his grandmother had *not* agreed upon was the "Irish Hour." David always thought that Maurice Seymour had a dumb speaking voice, that bagpipe music was sour and squawky, and that it was stupid to listen to dancers doing Irish steps on the radio when he couldn't see them and all you could hear was a lot of pounding and clumping around. He loved music but not bagpipe music. He preferred the music of Ben Bernie's orchestra, from the College Inn of the Hotel Sherman, or Bing Crosby's singing, or the voice of the hillbilly child Little Georgie Gobel on the WLS "Barn Dance" program. There were *some* pretty Irish songs, the slow ones like "My Wild Irish Rose," but fast Irish music played on bagpipes was dumb for sure.

In the kitchen Jack, Mike, O'Toole and Tommy Monaghan were all drinking beer.

"Jeez, Jack," Mike said, "it's too bad poor Joe isn't here to see us all together."

"Yeah," Jack said, "but it woulda killed him to see poor Ma lyin' in her coffin. He was her favorite, I guess. It's a good thing he died before *she* did. Good for him, I mean."

"How old was 'Seventy' when he died?" Tommy said, tilting his chair back.

"Let's see," Jack said. "He must have been—what—forty-five?"

The Wake

"At least," Mike said. "I know I was only twenty-two at the time."

"Why'd they call Joe *Seventy* in the first place?" O'Toole said.

"Because," Jack said, "when he was ten years old he had the wisdom of a man of seventy."

Mike laughed as he thought back over the years. "Jeez, Jack, do you remember—Joe was the comic at all the wakes in the old days. If they didn't have Joe there to tell 'em a few stories and sing a couple of songs, why, it wasn't a good wake at all."

"Yeah," Jack said. "He'd have us all dyin' laughin' in the kitchen. I remember at Packy Rafferty's funeral he got tired of hearing Packy's wife sayin' 'Poor Packy.' It was poor Packy this and poor Packy that, when Joe says he knew for a fact that Packy had beat the life out of her the night before he died. They were all in the parlor sayin' 'Poor Packy, there'll never be another like him,' and Joe was out in the kitchen saying, 'Sure, Packy's lucky he never got arrested.'"

They all laughed. "Yeah, I remember that myself," Mike said. "Rafferty's wake lasted three days and three nights in the worst heat of the summer and, by Jeez, by the time he was finally carried out the family was so glad to get rid of him they'd have dumped him out a window!"

"I don't remember the undertakers comin' round the house so much back in the old days," Tom Monaghan said.

"Oh, they dropped around from time to time," Mike said, "to see that the guest of honor didn't *melt*, I guess."

O'Toole chuckled. "Ah, those were the good old days," he said.

"It's funny," Jack said.

"What's that?" Tommy said.

"I was just thinking," Jack said, "we're always talking about the good old days. But when we were in the *middle* of 'em we didn't know they were that good."

"You're right," Mike said, swishing the beer in his glass into a spiral pool, "we miss the *old* days, and we're hopin' for some good news *tomorra*. Whatever happened to right now?"

"Well, now," O'Toole said, "the old days weren't always that good for *you*, were they, Mike?"

"Ah, hell," Mike said, "I just got in with some wrong guys, was all."

"Did you know Bugs Moran personally?" Tom asked.

"Hell, no. I had nothin' to do with him or O'Bannion or the rest o' them murderin' bastards. But I was pretty handy with my dukes in those days and when the newspapers was fightin', ya know, well, I picked up a little extra money keepin' certain street corners clear for one paper or the other. Helpin' to, I mean. I didn't do it all by myself, God knows."

"I never knew just how ya got in trouble," Tom said.

"Ah, I took a bum rap," Mike said. "It was Danny Ragen's fault. He was workin' for that son-of-a-bitch Annenberg and he gave some fella on the other side an awful beatin'. The poor bastard almost died. There was some witnesses, some old ladies lookin' out a winda, and they thought Ragen did it, but because him and me looked pretty much alike and was dressed alike, well, I took the rap for him."

"Why'd you do a thing like that?" O'Toole said.

"Well, hell, he had a wife and kids and besides one of Annenberg's guys promised me a bundle if I'd do it and said he'd pull a few strings and see to it that I'd get off with, you know, no time at all."

"So what did they hit ya with?"

"Six months. I did it standin' on one foot. But I never wanted to have anything to do with them bastards after that. I was always as ready as the next guy to get into a good fight, but I seen that the Irish was gonna lose out in this town anyway, no matter what."

"I thought the big shots was still runnin' things," O'Toole said.

"Oh, yeah. There's Bathhouse John and Hinky Dink and plenty more Irish thieves like 'em runnin' the wards and all. No, I mean gamblin' and booze and all that, where the real money is. In the old days O'Bannion and Bugs Moran and a lot of other Irish guys were takin' the big slice but hell, now it's gettin' to be all the Wops. And Big Bill Thompson is the biggest crook of them all. And Cermak is just as bad."

"Yeah, it's terrible the way Chicago is today," Monaghan said. "My brother Bill couldn't get into the Fire Department till he paid somebody, I think it was over five hundred dollars under the table. Just to get a job and do an honest day's work, for Christ's sake."

"God," O'Toole said. "That's great, isn't it? You got to pay off somebody in this town even to become a fireman or a copper. So how can there be any honest cops if they start you off as a crook before you can pick up your first pay check?"

"Yeah," said Mike. "There were good times in the old days, all right, but Chicago had nothin' to do with 'em. It was just whatever fun you could have with your friends."

David ran out of his bedroom, excited. "Aunt Maggie," he shouted, "it's Mama! I just saw the taxi out the window."

Margaret poked her head out of the bathroom. "Are you sure, honey?" she said.

"Yes!"

Josie hurried in from the parlor. "Ssshh! David, not so loud."

"It's my mama, Aunt Josie! She's home!"

"Now, Josie," Margaret called, "don't cause any trouble."

"*Me!*" Josie said. "If there's trouble it'll be *that* one."

"I'll get the door," Rose said, coming in from the parlor. She opened the door and, seeing no one, called down the stairs.

"Is that you down there, Belle? Yes, it's Belle, Maggie!"

David rushed through the door and into his mother's arms. "Mama!"

His mother was wearing a flashy but not stylish sealskin coat and a red felt hat. Her hair was peroxide blond, her lipstick bright red. She carried a red tricycle.

"Hello, sweetie," she said. "Oh, Mama Belle has missed her big boy so much! Look, Mama brought you a present!"

David looked down at the tricycle, observing at once that it was too small for him. "That's keen," he said, but his voice was not enthusiastic.

"Hello, Belle," Margaret said.

"Hello, Maggie," Belle said. "What's wrong, David. Don't you *like* the bike?"

"Oh, sure," David said, "but I'm kinda big for a three-wheeler."

She looked at him with sudden sarcastic contempt. "You *would!* And after the *fight* I had with the damned cab driver about gettin' the thing into the back seat. Well, ride it or not." She strode in, removing her coat.

"He'll love it, Belle," Margaret said. "Here, give me your coat." She helped to remove her sister's coat, then carried it to the closest bedroom.

At that moment Belle saw Josie, who had stepped forward. "Oh, hello, Josie."

"Hello, Belle."

"Where's Ma?" Belle said. She hurried into the parlor and to the coffin, beginning to weep. Slowly she shook her head from side to side as she looked down at her mother.

"Well, Bridget, it was finally too much for ya. Ah, God. Ma. She looks beautiful, Maggie."

Margaret had returned and now stood at Belle's side. "Yes, doesn't she. The poor old soul."

"God," Belle said, "I won't know what the word 'home' means any more, will you? Home always meant where Ma was."

"Well, you're always welcome here, Belle, Ma or no Ma. Welcome as the flowers in May, you know that. After all, little Dave is here."

"That's right," Belle said. "How has he been?" Seeing David again she said, "How have you been, sweetie?"

"Just as good as gold, Belle," Margaret said. "He's still his mama's boy, aren't you, honey?"

"I'll bet," Belle said sarcastically. "Now that Ma's dead, there's nobody to stick up for me in *this* house."

Josie, embarrassed, said, "Oh, Belle, you remember the McCaffrey sisters and Molly Fitzgerald, don't you?"

"Sure," Belle said. "Hello, Sarah—Molly. Mary, how are ya?"

"How are ya, Belle?" Sarah said. "You look grand. How's the show business?"

"We're sorry about poor Bridget, Belle," Mary McCaffrey said. "We was tellin' Maggie."

"Hello, Belle," Molly said.

"*Molly,* it's good to see you!" Belle said, turning.

"Gosh," Molly said, "you look the picture of health. Doesn't she look grand, Josie?"

"Yes," Josie said primly. "How long has your hair been that shade, Belle?"

"Why," Belle said touchily, "is there something wrong with it?"

"Oh, God," Josie said, rolling her eyes to heaven.

"Where is Doug Roberts, Mama?" David said. "Isn't *he* coming to Grandma's wake?"

"Never mind, honey," Margaret said, quickly. "Doug probably has to work."

"He only works with Mama Belle, doesn't he?" David said.

"He won't be able to make it, Davey," his mother said irritably. To Margaret she said, "Where are the boys?"

"They're out in the kitchen," Margaret said. "Jack got here all right."

"Oh, good," Belle said. "I'm anxious to see him."

"By the way," Margaret said, "you know Matty Mulcahey, Belle."

"Yes, hello, Belle," Matty said. "I'm sorry for your trouble. This is Chuck McDermott."

"We've met, Matty," Chuck said. "Belle and my sister Peggy worked together down at Florsheim's shoe factory—it must be—what?—twenty-five years ago, Belle."

"If it's a day," Belle said. "You haven't changed much, Chuck. It's good to see you."

"So sorry about your poor mother," Chuck said.

"Thank you," Belle said. "Wait till I say a prayer." She knelt and prayed silently.

Margaret put her arm on David's shoulder and led him into the dining-room area. "Oh, Davey, by the way, honey— don't mention Doug Roberts to either Uncle Mike or Uncle Jack, okay?"

"Why not?" David said. "Don't they like him?"

"Never mind. Just remember what I'm telling you."

"All right," he said. "But I like him. Aunt Maggie, why can't all the people *I* love—love each other?"

Margaret hugged him suddenly. "I don't know. Listen, we're outta milk. Run down to the A&P and get me two quarts, will you, like a good boy?" She picked up her purse from a sideboard. "Here's a quarter. Be sure to bring home the change."

"All right."

"And be sure to put on your sweater."

"Aunt Mag," David said, "if Mama Belle and Doug

Roberts get married—which would make him my dad—*then* would Uncle Mike and Uncle Jack like him?"

"That wouldn't make him your dad, honey. Your father died when you were a baby—you know that. That would make him your *step*father. But never mind. Run along now, like a good boy."

David got his sweater and moved to the door, encountering his mother and Rose. "I'm going to the store, Mama. I'll be right back."

"All right, sweetie," Belle said.

"Button your sweater up all the way," Rose said. "It's chilly out."

"I will."

"Belle," Rose said, whispering, "I'm goin' outta my mind for a cigarette."

"Are the boys in the kitchen, did Maggie say?"

"Yeah. They're out there talking to some of the old gang."

"Here," Belle said, "I've got some Luckies. You got a match?" She fumbled in her purse.

"I'll go to the kitchen and get some matches for you, Mama," David said, starting down the hall.

"No, Davey!" Rose said. "Don't go *near* the kitchen!"

"Why not?"

"Well," his mother said, "uh—Uncle Mike is funny about women smoking, honey. So don't say anything to him about Aunt Rose and me havin' a cigarette, all right?"

"Okay."

"Come on, Belle," Rose said. "The coast is clear in the

toilet. We can go in there and smoke." They stepped into the bathroom and locked the door.

In the kitchen the men were still drinking beer. "Jack, even though the rest of us had the wanderlust," Mike said, "all but poor Mag, I guess . . . I think you're the only one of us that *really* got away. Now, why should that be, I wonder?"

"How did I get away?" Jack said. "I'll be damned if I know. Well, I was the only one that went to high school and all that, but it can't be that simple."

"Jesus, there's plenty in this town that did that much and still ended up doin' time at Joliet," Mike said.

"You ought to know, eh?" O'Toole said, laughing.

"That's right," Jack said. "No, Mike, I don't really know what it was. There was always something pushin' me, it seemed. It made me get a little more schoolin' than the rest of you. And then, when I got to France during the war, when I saw a bit of the world—I don't know, I was only eighteen but I came to realize that even if Chicago is one of the biggest towns in the world it's still just a tiny black dot on the map, ya know? So I had this idea there was an awful lot out there to see, and something in me just had to see it."

"Funny," Mike said, lighting a home-rolled Bull Durham cigarette, "I had the same feelin', in a way. I mean about wantin' to see the world, but I never saw any more of it than California and Texas and Minnesota and a few other odd places. And not much more of *them* than you could see from the railyards or the nearest flophouse. But the main thing about you, Jack, is that you *made* somethin' of yourself, when the rest of us was sittin' around here doin' the same damned things year after year."

"Well, hell, that's the breaks too, Mike. I never figured a man deserves any credit for doing what he *has* to do. I just went with the wind, was all. So I had a knack with words and I wrote a couple of books. So what? I didn't give myself the knack any more than I gave myself blue eyes."

"I wonder what it was," O'Toole said, "the thing you said was pushin' ya?"

"Damned if I know," Jack said. "Maybe—maybe it was just a desire to break loose of the ties that held me down when I was home here."

"Couldn't you have cut 'em loose without leavin' town?" Mike said.

"I doubt it, Mike. I think maybe we never can *cut* ties of that kind. Maybe the reason I went so far away is that I knew I couldn't cut 'em and I thought that if I got a million miles away I'd stretch 'em so far they'd *break*."

"Did they?" O'Toole said, tapping out the ashes from his pipe.

"Some did. Some didn't."

"Jeez," Mike said. "I wonder if that's what the old man had in mind—takin' off like he did and leavin' us all here alone."

"Oh, don't sound so sorry for yourself," Jack said. "You were sixteen when he left. That's old enough to stand on your own two feet. Jesus, I used to blame the old man for hittin' the road back to Ireland—I used to hate him, in fact. But I got over that. What the hell did he have to keep him

here? A bunch of crazy kids that wouldn't listen to a word
he said. Two of the girls ran off as soon as they could scrape
up enough money for a railroad ticket—and Joe was doin'
time at Joliet, the rest hittin' the bottle. What'd he have to
keep him here except . . . *obligations.* He wanted Ma to go
with him, you know that. But she wouldn't." He drained a
glass of beer. There was a long pause.

"Jack," Mike said, "do you ever think of goin' back to the
Church?"

"Mike," Jack said, "do you ever think of goin' back to
work?" They all laughed.

On the way to the store David avoided stepping on the
straight lines that separated the rectangles of concrete, saying to himself, "Step on a crack, break your mother's back."

Crossing 49th Street he looked into the shopwindows, at
the displays which never ceased to fascinate him. There were
small laundries, dry cleaners, garages, bakeries, groceries,
saloons, plumbers, all with their wares and advertisements in
the windows.

A bright red streetcar flashed by, roaring and clacking,
scattering small whirls of dust and paper tatters behind it.
From somewhere blocks away he could hear the soft slow
choo . . . choo . . . choo . . . of a train just getting under
way. It was one of his favorite sounds.

Now that his mother was home there would be a wonderful trip somewhere, he felt, very soon, to the magic anywhere-
but-here, hopefully made on a train. Trains were sad when
you only heard them from a distance in the night, making

their long, mournful cry, but they were wonderful when you were on them. He remembered clearly the stiff, dark green velvetlike upholstery of the Pullman cars, the crisp, white linen in the diners, the friendly, smiling Negro waiters, the frightening, thrilling view from the back platform of the observation cars at the end of the train, at the ends of all the passenger trains in the world.

Sleeping on a train was the most delicious feeling of all. He remembered waking up on some train on a night long past, warm under the covers in the lower berth, quivering from excitement and the chill that went through him when he pressed his hands and nose against the ice-cold window through which he could see lanterns moving, and workmen who looked like Martian gnomes as they lurched past, calling to each other, waving their gloved hands.

The train was just pulling into a station—or was it pulling out?—a little depot in a small town, and by the dim light from the old building he could see snow on the ground, steam rushing up from under the car he was in, and the wisps of vapor coming from the mouths of strangers who slipped past slowly in the darkness.

He loved the feeling when a train was sitting motionless in a station, and suddenly either the train he was on or the one next to it, on another track, began to move. At first you couldn't tell whether it was your train or the other one that was moving.

He remembered once when, the previous winter, he had accidentally performed the same trick with the entire earth. He had been standing under a street lamp during a heavy snowfall. The flakes were large and falling thickly, straight down, and there came a moment when it seemed that the millions of flakes were motionless, white blobs of paint on a black canvas, and it was himself and the whole planet, magnetized to the bottoms of his feet, that were floating softly, airily upward.

Jack walked into the old familiar bathroom to relieve himself and stood for a moment, looking about. It was, like most of the other rooms in the house, somehow sad-looking, and yet it provided the members of the family a sense of homeness. There was the slowly dripping faucet in the ancient tub with its painted dragon feet, the plain twine stretched over the tub, to hang wet clothing on, the cheap lace curtains over the cracked and spotted yellow shade, the ancient tan paint on the walls, the medicine cabinet with its false-teeth powders, its laxatives—Nujol, Pluto water, Ex-Lax, Feen-a-mint and Phillips Milk of Magnesia.

He inspected the shelves of the cabinet, looking for an aspirin, without luck. There was a wrinkled tube of Ipana toothpaste, a small bottle of Vaseline hair tonic, a larger bottle containing a dark brown tonic called "Beef, Iron and Wine," an unopened bar of Lifebuoy soap, a small bottle of Pine Tar Compound, a bitter black liquid that could be swallowed only by sprinkling a few drops of it on a spoonful of sugar, a small bottle of Listerine, a bottle of hydrogen peroxide, a tiny eyecup of brilliant blue glass, a small box of Sen-Sen, a bottle of Jergen's lotion, an orange package of Smith

Brothers' cough drops, a bottle of Rem cough syrup, a small blue jar of Vicks VapoRub salve, some Gem razor blades, and a brown bottle of Lysol. The cabinet did not seem to have changed in any noticeable particular for the past twenty years. All the small objects in the house seemed strangely constant: the small, red tomato pincushion on the sideboard in the dining room, the bowl of wax fruit—apples, banana, peach, orange—the washboard left in the tub, with a bar of Fels-Naphtha soap perched on its upper shelf, the picture of the Sacred Heart of Jesus in the hall, in the kitchen the calendar from an insurance company, the iceman's sign, the cracked oilcloth on the kitchen table, the Spanish shawl draped randomly over the dining-room table, the cheap Arabian "rug" on a side table, the copies of *Our Sunday Visitor*, *Liberty* and *The Saturday Evening Post* in a wooden magazine rack, the sewing basket on the sideboard, with its multicolored spools and shiny thimbles, the red metal candy box that now held assorted buttons, the Majestic radio in the dining room and the smaller Atwater Kent in the front bedroom. And, here and there about the house, bunion pads.

After a few minutes, suddenly tired from two days on trains and the nervous strain of it all, he decided to go into one of the bedrooms and lie down for a while. The front bedroom was empty. He lowered its window shade and stretched out.

Looking at the old, familiar tan-cream ceiling, with its tracery of cracks, he felt at the same time both a stranger and at home. There was something comforting to the physical part of him about being back with all of them again, back with the faces, the talk, the food, the smells, the furniture, the wallpapers, the neighborhood scenes. But his mind felt as if it had returned from a journey of a million miles rather than a thousand. What in God's name did they use their own minds for? They were all simple animal functions, prejudices, modest pleasures, local concerns: ball scores and murders and scandals. They had a little interest in the popular music they heard on the radio, and the Church, of course, but other than that, nothing. No art, no sculpture, no literature, no philosophy, no poetry, no science, no history; in a word: no culture.

Uprooted as a people by forces they could not even identify, much less interpret, they no longer even knew anything about their own historical and geographical background. To them the image of the home country was the word IRELAND, printed in bright green on tasteless St. Patrick's Day cards and advertisements. It was all an empty jumble of shamrocks, pictures of St. Patrick himself, golden harps, songs like "Mother Machree," "Little Town in the Ould County Down," and "Danny Boy," pointless prejudice against Protestants and—and—that was about the size of it. All meaningless bits and pieces: The Fighting Irish of Notre Dame—who were mostly Poles, Czechs and Italians—and Pat O'Brien in the movies, and boasts about John L. Sullivan and the "Irish Hour" on the radio and nowhere anything at the center. They were so estranged from their past, he thought, that it was doubtful if they would even remember having heard of Finn MacCool, Charles Parnell, Henry Grattan, Henry Flood, Wolfe Tone, Lord Edward Fitzgerald, Robert Emmet and the rest. And as for the literary luminaries

of the land—Thomas Moore, Thomas Parnell, Sir Richard
Steele, Jonathan Swift, Yeats, Shaw, Synge, Sheridan,
O'Casey, Joyce—he knew these names would mean no more
to them than the names of African tribesmen.

On the wall his gaze fell upon a colored picture of Christ
holding a white lamb in his arms. *Agnus Dei, qui tollis*
peccata mundi. For a moment he thought back to the Latin
of the Mass he had never pressed on to qualify himself to
say, but still remembered. Half asleep now he saw himself
blessing a congregation, wearing a golden chasuble trimmed
with red, then holding the ciborium. Again the lamb on the
wall. *Agnus Dei, qui tollis peccata mundi.* Lamb of God,
who takest away the sins of the world. *Miserere nobis . . .*
dona nobis pacem. Grant us peace.

Dominus vobiscum.

Et cum spirito tuo.

It seemed to Jack that for peace of spirit the three best
times were when he was waking up, when he was falling
asleep, and when the second drink had begun to affect him.
Drunkenness did not appeal to him, but the first faint glow
of alcohol did. Certain matters and questions became clear to
him then that not only were not clear at other times but did
not even exist for him.

To be sure they were not very important things. One April
morning in Boston, with the window open, he had heard a
shovel scraping in the street and workmen's voices quietly
joking. For a time he listened to the sounds in his sleep and
they became wound up in his dreams. Then for a few
minutes he lay quietly awake, listening. He heard one man

laugh loudly and say, "I thought you said you knew how to *run* that thing."

It was not an extraordinarily cruel thing to say, but lying there half awake Jack Scanlan felt what cruelty there was to it and winced in sympathy with the anonymous victim to whom the subtle, joking insult was directed. There was cruelty all day long, unrecognized. "Say, you're putting on a little weight, aren't you?"

"I distinctly *told* you I wanted *three* carbons, not two."

"Don't get me wrong, there's nothing *wrong* with your wearing high-heeled shoes to my mother's party."

Moving fast through the stream of disguised invective you could scarcely notice it sinking into the flesh of its targets. But lying still and half awake, it was evident, brushing against your own face, in a sense tangible.

The matter of degree puzzled him. He could grasp the extremes easily enough. Cruelty and kindness. War and peace. Good and evil. Up and down. Hot and cold. Heaven and hell. No, even the extremes were a problem. How carefully could you back up from peace before you found yourself at war? How slowly could you move, measuring your progress with delicate instruments, moving away from the complete good, through the relative good, and the less good, before you discovered that you were surrounded by evil? It was like the question: Can you step anyway but south when you're standing on the North Pole?

Another idea he had when half asleep. Could you devise a chart of the spectrum, relating the colors to virtues and vices? Of course, but it would be worthless. Or of course you could not. Unless perhaps you wanted to try it anyway. He sometimes had the feeling that great truths were just barely eluding him when he was falling asleep. If only he had the energy to wake up fully and make some notes, he used to think. And then in the next minute the elusive truths were part of his dreams and such commotion there was then!

A week earlier he had fallen asleep and had a dream that for all its strangeness was well known to him. Though he had first experienced it as a child, the meaning of it had never been made plain to him. The dream was a sharp conflict of physical moods rather than the usual tangle of fantastic events and time-whipped statements and faces. It represented a struggle between all that was lovely numb-warm smoothness and all that was stark, nail-scraping jagged roughness. First as he slept a soft distant hum would begin in the far timeless black corners of his mind, seeming to originate in some large round rolling object, a wheel or a ball. Never had there been such a comforting feeling of frictionless tranquillity as that induced by the untroubled rolling and low humming of the perfectly smooth wheel or ball. It was obscured in half darkness and its dimensions could not be precisely perceived, but a polished metal sphere rolling down a slight incline on a surface of gossamer, oiled silk or velvet might be said to represent in physical form this idea—ideal?—of lubricated and free passage that the dream's vague imagery created in his mind. It felt warm and good. Very good.

Then with a vibrating, whooshing and threatening onrush, with an ominous growling, a muffled whine, the spirit of *conflict* would suddenly flicker from the heart of the ball of peace, which would develop jagged, tormented sandpaper protuberances on its outer wall. These would rip into and catch on the smooth surface over which it had been rolling. But now it could no longer be said to be rolling for its flight had become crazed and irregular and it bumped and scraped monstrously along, seeming to grind, clatter and rattle the very foundations of the universe itself. For long wild minutes his mind was a seething, screeching, maddened scene of vast hollowness and red darkness, of chaos filled with the grumble of machinery, the scream of tortured metallic surfaces, and the maniacal abandon of matter dedicated to exposing itself destructively to abrasive friction.

But the most strikingly peculiar and mysterious thing about the dream was that even in the most frenzied, panicky moments of its friction phase there was still evident, in the background, the original omnipresent sensation of oil-smooth, free passage, the delicious, warm sensation of blasé comfort, the security represented by that same original luscious hum of smoothness, that same primal mood of heavy-lidded tranquillity. In these moments when conflict and peace incongruously shared the stage of his mind he felt discomfort but no fear, rather a magnificent confidence that he was in no true danger and that warmth, stillness and languor would shortly reassume sole command of the scene.

He felt no emotional involvement (or at best very little) with the action that occurred in his dream and soon, before a minute had passed (or what seemed to be a minute and what actually might have been the flicker of time's eyelash), his confidence would be rewarded by a gradual lessening of confusion, a slowing and weakening of the dynamos, a sudden overcoming of the disturbing forces that had disrupted his original isolated composure. And, as the dream came to its blind close, comfort would be restored, contentment would remount the throne, and he would feel at peace.

As a child he was familiar with this psychic phenomenon only in dreams but as a young adult he had begun to meet it face to face while wide awake. Even then he had not been in any way frightened or confused. Rather he was fascinated by the curious and exciting physical manifestation of the state. It always came to him when he was alone, rather tired, and sitting or lying in silence in the late hours of the night. He would be reading in an easy chair or perhaps propped up on a pillow in bed. His concentration would suddenly become sidetracked by a mood of utter but addle-brained tranquillity and almost imperceptibly something would happen to upset his physical relationship to time and space. Actions that he would normally think of as taking two or three seconds to perform would seem now to take three or four times that long. If he flipped the page of a book it would not seem to be the normal quick flickering action but would appear to be an extremely slow and deliberate operation. If he lifted his hand to scratch his ear the hand—grown larger—seemed to take a mysteriously long time to reach his head; the scratching was a ponderous action, like that of a prehistoric giant beast scraping a tree bole. If he dropped the hand to his lap or his side the arm seemed to topple slowly, magnificently, like a tree in the forest.

As for spatial relations generally they were thrown wildly

off kilter. Objects appeared larger than they in fact were. His hands were giant, fleshy, the fingers as thick as wrists. Strangely, objects did not so much *look* larger, they just *felt* larger. A newspaper page, when turned, crackled and waved as if it were three times normal size and made of an almost metallic, crinkly, rattly material. There was a sort of slow-motion majesty to things that seemed to be directly related to the over-all sensation of confidence, smoothness and relaxation that always characterized the first part of the dream state. Then, as he always expected, just as when he was asleep, the friction phase would introduce itself and the world would begin to crash and tumble and grind.

Unseen lightning crackled and roared through the million mileness in his head. If he ran his fingernails through his hair at such moments the nails contacted the scalp with much loud scraping and ponderous activity. If he coughed the sound echoed slowly, like a cannon fired under water. If he smiled his facial muscles gathered themselves together very deliberately and at last finally contrived to lift the corners of his mouth, which felt unusually large and heavy. If he stood up he felt like a great robot, full of hinges and pulleys and intricately balanced so as not to fall down. If he walked across a room he was Gargantua, striding waist-deep through a wide sea.

Through all this the battle between the rough and the smooth still raged. He could terminate the experience at any moment at will by simply shaking himself and clearing his head, but he never did, and eventually he learned to prolong the feeling by keeping his movements to a minimum, the better to observe his reactions and sensations.

Finally, after perhaps five or ten minutes, his mind would clear with no exercise of the will and life would go on as before.

He had talked to several people about the experience and could find no one but Hilda, an earlier love, who understood what he was talking about. She told him that the first time she had undergone the experience it had frightened her badly and that she had feared she was losing her mind. He could never fully understand his own wanting to prolong the feeling. He knew only that the sensation could be brought on by a combination of fatigue and quiet surroundings, but he was never able to learn more about it. One time a jazz musician he knew, a saxophone player who often wore dark glasses, even during the day, described the sensation of smoking marijuana and when he said, "Time seems to slow right down and you can play an awful lot of notes, and they're important notes," Jack felt a flicker of recognition. But he would never know.

CHAPTER FOUR

When she heard the doorbell, Josie, who was the closest, answered it. A delivery boy stood before her, carrying a floral piece.

"Flowers for Bridget Scanlan," he said.

"Who's at the door?" Rose called, from down the hall.

"It's more flowers for Ma," Josie said, showing the boy in.

"Put 'em in there," Rose said, following Josie into the parlor. She walked with the boy to the coffin and, after he had positioned the flowers, gave him a tip. When he had left Rose looked at the card on the flowers.

"Who are them flowers from, Rose?" Josie said.

"None of your business."

"What do you mean, none of my business? I asked you a civil question."

"Oh, you did, eh?"

"That's right, I did," Josie said, her face reddening.

"Well, the flowers are from Doug Roberts, if you have to know."

"Oh," Josie said, "you might know it."

"Listen," Rose said, "the way Bella lives her life is her own business, not yours."

"I don't care how she lives her life, but I don't want flowers from that man here in front of Ma's coffin."

"Oh, shut up," Rose snapped.

"You shut up yourself, Rose. And don't raise your voice to me. Don't you have any respect for the dead? What would Ma think—flowers from that man in this house!"

"Listen, what Ma would think is her own business. The flowers stay right where they were. In fact, they're kinda pretty."

"Oh, sure," Josie said, "stick up for him."

"I'm not stickin' up for anybody. I'm just saying Duffy the florist woulda sent these damned flowers over no matter who paid for 'em, and it can't do a Goddamned bit of harm to have them here. We can take the name tag offa the thing if you're so worried about it."

Josie rushed to her in great fury, then passed to the coffin, crying, "Oh, Ma, Ma. What are they doin' to ya? Ma!"

Rose left her sister Josie at the coffin. Walking along the hallway she said, mostly to herself, "God, that Josie!"

"What's the matter?" Belle called from the bathroom.

Her sister gave her the high sign that it was nothing that could be discussed in the presence of Jack and Mike. "Oh, nothin'," she said. "That Josie gets crazier every day. I wish to hell she'd stayed in California. She thinks she's too damned good for us, I guess." As they reached the kitchen, Rose said, "Jack—Mike. Belle's here."

"It's good to see you, sister," Jack said, shaking her hand.

"You too, Jack," Belle said.

The Wake

"Hello, Belle. How are ya?" Mike said. They all hated hellos and good-bys and were no good at them.

"Fine, Mike," Belle said. "How are you?"

"Holdin' up. What were you just sayin' about Josie, Rose?"

"Nothin'."

"Ah, don't listen to her, Rosie," Belle said.

"Jesus, Mary and Joseph," Mike said, "can't you two leave Josephine alone? She hasn't set foot in this house for over five years and right off the bat you two are causin' her trouble! Can't you be peaceable just until poor Ma is in her grave?"

"Ah, come on, Jack, Tommy," Mike said, "let's go out in the back yard for a breath of fresh air, outside where it's peaceful. Belle, we'll see you in a few minutes."

Jack stood looking at Belle for a moment. The corners of her mouth were pursed in the familiar expression of paranoid tension and distrust. Mike's unexpected attack had unsettled her.

"How's the world been treatin' ya, sister?" Jack said, smiling hopefully.

"Fine, fine, Jack," she said, toying aimlessly with a worn spot on the table's oilcloth. Then, "I thought you'd come see me when I played Boston last winter."

"I did," Jack said very quietly. "I was out front the night you closed. You were terrific."

"Well, good God," she said, "why didn't you come back stage?"

"I stayed to see the damned movie and when I went back to the stage door they told me you'd already checked out."

"God," she said bitterly, "we have a lot of luck, don't we?"

"Yeah," he sighed, and then squared his shoulders. "Belle, I want to talk to you about Davey."

She tensed. "Listen," she said, "can't it wait? I've got a splitting headache."

"Oh, all right, Belle," he said. "I'll talk to you later." He joined the other men on the back porch.

"Rose, what were you sayin' about Josie?" Belle asked, to change the subject.

"Oh, never mind."

"No, tell me. What is it?"

"It's nothin'—some flowers just arrived from Doug Roberts and when Josie saw who they were from she threw a fit."

Jumping up, Belle said, "Oh, she *did*, did she? Well, I'll tell her to mind her own Goddamned business once and for all."

"No, Belle, sit down. I already told her what I thought of her. She's in there with Ma now, crying and blabbering like she's not in her right mind. Leave her alone."

"Well, it's none of her business if Doug wants to send flowers, although I might have known that horse's ass would do something like this."

"What's wrong with what he did?" Rose said.

"Well, you can see what it caused."

"Never mind. What do you care?"

"No, I do care," Belle said, pacing the floor. "Oh, I'll give him *hell* when I see him."

"So now you're on Josie's side, huh?"

"No, damn her. It's none of her business what Doug Roberts does."

"I already *told* her that. So let Ma be in peace and don't go in there now and start a fight."

"Say, Rose, is there a drink in the house?"

"I think Maggie keeps a drop hidden away somewhere."

"God, I wish I knew where it was. I'm goin' outta my mind with nerves."

"But, Belle, don't start drinkin' now. If the boys see that you've had a drop they'll kill you. Or they'll kill me for givin' it to you."

"Then you know where it is?"

"No, I don't. She used to keep it in the top cupboard there, over the sink, layin' down on its side so ya couldn't see it, but I don't think it's there any more. Listen, you just relax here for a few minutes and I'll go in and apologize to Josie, if I have to. Anything to shut her up." As she left she clenched her fist. "Oh, I could kill her!" she said.

Belle stood for a moment looking out the window over the sink. The view was of a gloomy brick wall and the slim branches of a young tree, the leaves moving gently in the autumn breeze. It reminded her of a similar view once seen from a side window of a cheap hotel in Kansas, during a dust storm. She and Doug had driven their 1929 Chevy through the ominous, gathering clouds of dry death, on the way to Tulsa and points west. Finally it had become too dark and gusty to go farther and they had put up for the night in a now-forgotten two-story hotel in an unmemorable town.

She did not understand the sober-faced farmers and small merchants she saw in such places. They were the same as foreigners. But she felt sorry for them, with their poor-looking overalls and worn hats, their dry faces, their defeated eyes. In towns medium-sized and large, across the face of the land, such people and the others who made up America—the Southerners, the hillbillies, the Westerners, the hicks and the big-city types—were in the aggregate just the audience. She could handle them on that basis. But as individuals, with their strange ways and wary eyes, they seemed a breed apart. She felt most at home with the rounders, the carnival, vaudeville types, the comics, straight men, singers, musicians, managers, stagehands, and those with whom they associated; the saloon owners, the bartenders, the bellboys, the con men, the gamblers, the looser, freer people. She wished at this moment that she was with them, having fun, having a few drinks, a few laughs. The need for a drink hit her hard then and she pulled a chair over to the counter above which Rose had said a bottle might be hidden.

There was nothing on the first shelf, nor on the second. Standing on tiptoe she felt among the cups, saucers and bowls on the third and then said silently, "Thank God," as her fingers touched a bottle, lying on its side.

With an added effort she got a grip on it and lowered it to eye level.

"Dago Red," she said in disgust. Well, it was better than nothing. She was still standing on the chair, taking a deep drink when, without her hearing, David opened the screen door and stepped into the room.

86

"Hi, Mama."

Her heart jumped as she hastily tried to hide the bottle.

"Oh," she said. "You scared me, sweetie." Stepping down from the chair she placed the bottle on its side and draped a dish towel over it, covering the movement as best she could with her body.

"Mama," David said, "you're not gonna get drunk today, are you?"

"Why," she said, forcing a nervous smile, "what are you talking about? Don't talk silly. That was just a little *medicinal* drink, to steady my nerves. What have you got there, sweetie?"

"Aunt Maggie sent me for a couple of bottles of milk," he said. He withdrew the bottles from the brown paper bag and put them into the icebox, close up against the fast-fading block of ice.

"Oh, that's right," Belle said. "That's a good boy."

"Mama," David said, "in a few days . . . when you leave . . . can I go with you? Can I come live with you again?"

She felt angry and helpless. "Honey," she said, "don't you love your Aunt Mag?"

"Yes. But she's not my mother. Why can't I go with you, Mama Belle?"

"Well, sweetie, it's mainly because you have to go to school. Before you started first grade it was all right if I dragged you with me on the road, but now you've got to get an education."

"Why?"

87

"Because that's the way things are, that's all. You don't want to grow up to be a dunce, do you?"

"I won't."

"I know you won't, sweetie, but all the other little boys you know have to go to school. That's just the way things are."

"Yeah, but all the other boys I know live with their mothers and fathers."

"But, Davey, don't you see—with your father dead I have to earn a living. *Somebody* has to pay for your support, your clothes, the food you eat. I pay for every penny of your support here."

"Well, can't you earn a living here in Chicago?"

"Oh, for a little while I could, yes. I do get some bookings around here, you know that. But most of the time I'm on the road. I have to work in New York or California or down South or someplace so I can make the money to send back here to Maggie, to buy you all the nice things you need."

"Now that Grandma's dead, who'll stay with me during the day? Aunt Mag doesn't get home from work till after six."

"Oh, God," his mother said, sighing and wringing her hands, "I hadn't thought of that. Well, we'll figure out something."

"What are Uncle Mike and Uncle Jack doing out on the back porch?"

"Getting some fresh air, I guess. It sure didn't take 'em long to walk out when I walked in. Some welcome. Listen,

Uncle Mike is usually here in the afternoon when you get home from school, isn't he?"

"Yeah. But every so often he gets drunk and has a big fight and then he has to go away . . . everybody in this family is always going away."

Belle felt unable to take any more of the conversation. "Yeah," she said. "Listen, your uncles'll catch their death of cold out there. Go tell 'em to come on in here where it's warm and cozy. I have to talk to your Aunt Rose a minute about the funeral arrangements."

David stared after her then glumly thrust his hands into his pockets. In the left pocket he could feel two nickels, a cap from a bottle of Green River pop, a handkerchief and a single blue marble. He took the marble out and looked at it solemnly, his mind floating back to his first recollection of it, when he had accidentally dropped it while eating dinner at a boarding school called St. Joseph's and it had fallen into a sauce dish full of chocolate pudding.

The boy next to him had laughed and then, just to be funny, to make the boy laugh again, David had pretended not to know that the marble was in the dish, had deliberately picked up a spoonful of pudding with the marble in it, and had put it into his mouth. Because the boy had laughed even more David pretended to swallow the marble with the mouthful of pudding.

It had fallen because he had been carrying it in the pocket of his khaki shirt, which was at the same time half full of salt. It was a thing all the children did whenever the nuns

served boiled spareribs for lunch or dinner. You licked two
or three of the rib bones till they were perfectly clean, then
you put them into the pocket of your khaki uniform shirt,
put a lot of salt into the pocket and then, later during the
day or evening, you could take the salty bones out and suck
on them if you felt hungry and it was too late to get anything to eat in the refectory.

He was not sure why he had saved the marble and still
carried it with him. For the most part the memories it revived
were unpleasant, a jumbled kaleidoscope of pomegranates
given out on Sunday and sucked for their red juice, of the
green glass from ginger-ale bottles pounded carefully with
a small rock until the glass had been reduced to a precious
pale-green magic powder, of running his hand along a
wooden wall rail and becoming almost delirious with pain
when a long splinter had been driven under the middle nail
of his right hand, of a wine-red Dodge driven by somebody
else's father coming to visit, of being sick and spending days
in the infirmary, with time terribly slowed and days and
nights that never seemed to end, of getting caught out of bed,
or just talking or giggling, on so many nights in the dormitory
and being made to stand in the corner, during the night,
shivering for what seemed like hours, while the other children fell asleep, of hearing the long, low sweet scream of
trains across distant green fields in the night, faintly smelling
the exciting smoke from their engines when, minutes later,
it drifted over the sleeping school.

He remembered dark green things at the school: the
avocados sent from California by a rich child's parents, and

hard green unripe pears stolen from a tree in the orchard behind the gymnasium, and the linoleum steps, four flights of them, that the boys had to polish sometimes on weekends or as extra punishment for long-forgotten crimes.

That was when he had begun to save things, stamps torn from letters, bottle caps, his teeth as they fell out, baseball cards with pictures of Max Bishop and Carl Hubbell and Lou Gehrig and the rest. He had been down to just a handful of marbles one day and then he had rolled the blue one at the target marble that sat on the floor between the outstretched legs of Fat Carl, whose father never came to see him. He had scored a clean hit and so it was his turn to sit down and for a long time nobody hit the blue marble and when they finally did he was able to stuff his pockets and marble bag with all the marbles, seemingly hundreds of them, that had come in because five other boys were rolling at once.

Rather than get back into the game and risk losing all his new-found fortune he had just walked away and for a long time after that he had had quite a lot of marbles, including the beautiful light blue one, which he had saved.

Rolling it in his palm now he remembered the time he had held a grasshopper on the open palm of the same hand and it had spit "tobacco juice" on him and then jumped away. The feeling had made his stomach crawl but to act tough in front of his friends he had pretended that it did not bother him.

The year at the school had come as a surprise and shock to him. He had thought that he was going far away with his mother but she had taken him only as far as La Grange and then they had gotten off the train. They had lunch at a tea shop near a small movie theatre, after which they had gotten into a taxi and driven out along a pleasant country road that eventually brought them to a series of large gray buildings that immediately looked to David like a prison.

"What place is this?" he had asked.

"It's St. Joseph's, honey," his mother had said.

"Why are we here?"

"Well," she said, "this is that surprise I was telling you about. See what a beautiful place it is? Well, it's just full of a lot of wonderful boys and I know you'll have a great time playing with all of them."

He started to cry then, still in the taxi, and said, "I want to go home."

"Don't worry, lady," the cab driver said, when he helped his mother carry the suitcases up the steps of the main building, "they all act like that when we drive 'em out here the first time."

"I don't want to go to this place, Mama," he said. "Please don't make me go here."

"But, honey," she said, "it isn't going to be forever. You see, I have to work in different parts of the country for a while, quite a few weeks, you know, and then—you'll see— I'll come back and visit you and—"

"Mama," he said, stiffening, "I don't want to be here. Don't go away and leave me here."

At that two nuns had come out of the building.

"Mrs. Considine?" the older one said.

His mother was crying. She was trying to smile, to make

him feel better, but he could tell that she was getting angry, too. He broke away and ran down the steps, back to the cab. The nuns said something to his mother and patted her on the back, then the three women walked slowly toward him, the two nuns smiling gently. The nuns took his hands and then his arms as his mother hurried into the cab. The driver rode away fast, the tires of the cab throwing up little pieces of gravel as he sped around the curved driveway then out through the gates and leftward, onto the road back toward town.

The nuns tried to talk to him but he insisted on watching the yellow cab until it was only a small spot of color through the distant greenery.

He remembered it all now, and much more, but this time, he was sure, his mother would not leave him.

He walked to the screen door and stood for a moment looking out at his Uncle Mike and the other men on the back porch. He had no conscious recollection of his father, just the memory of snapshots in the family album—a tall, good-looking man, usually smiling, and in some of the pictures holding David himself, as a baby, in his arms. There were pictures in back yards, on beaches, a few—eight by tens—in vaudeville poses and many, with groups of strangers in railroad stations, beside trains. In some of them his father had a mustache but in almost all of them he was smiling.

"Your father was a sweetheart," he was frequently told. "He was a mighty good-natured fella."

"He always looked on the bright side of things," his Aunt Mag had told him. "Everybody loved Billy Considine."

That the Scanlans had an unequivocal good word to say for anybody was remarkable enough to David so he gladly accepted the many compliments he had heard paid to his father. Together with the photographs they made up the only impression of him that he had—a tall, smiling, well-liked man. But the impression was too much like that of someone he had only heard about or read about and so his Uncle Mike, faults and all, served as a more real father substitute. As mean as he frequently was to the others in the family he had never said a cruel word to David. There was Uncle Jack but for all his post cards he had been almost as hazy a figure in David's mind, over the years, as his father. Uncle Jack was "away," though David rarely knew where.

But Mike was around the house frequently, particularly since he was almost invariably out of work. David was never precisely sure just what work he was out of but it seemed to have something to do with trains. Uncle Charlie, Aunt Rose's husband, worked for the Illinois Central, but he went to work every day and David had heard him discussing his specific duties with the rest of the family. It had something to do with lots of freight cars, switching them around in the yards and keeping track of them. But with Uncle Mike he was never sure.

Mike, too, would go away from time to time and sometimes months would pass before he returned. Now and then David was told that he was at a soldiers' home, in Danville, Illinois, or at West Allis, Wisconsin. Sometimes he would just go away, period, and none of the women in the family seemed to have any idea where he was.

"I'm worried sick," Grandma Scanlan would say. "We haven't heard from Mike in eight weeks."

"Oh, don't worry, Ma," Mag would say. "He'll turn up. If anything had happened to him we would have heard about it."

Mag would be just as worried as Grandma or Aunt Rose but the women would take turns cheering each other up. They were all confirmed pessimists but usually not at the same time. Whichever one picked up the pessimism first seemed to have a claim on it. The others would automatically assume the optimistic role, though rarely with a great deal of conviction.

Sure enough, Mike would turn up eventually, usually in an oddly quiet or withdrawn mood. He would smile at David but otherwise would walk slowly about the house, sigh a great deal, read the papers, make himself an occasional cigarette, look out the window, listen to the radio, cut himself shaving, put little pieces of toilet paper on the cuts, drink a great deal of coffee, and gradually get more and more irritable. Finally he would have a loud argument with his mother and sisters and would storm out of the house, slamming the door. Then, several hours later, almost inevitably, he would come home drunk.

Sometimes, when he was away from home for a long time, they would get a letter from him. It was always written on cheap, dime-store narrow stationery, lined. It was never more than one page long and it usually began "Dear Sister." It was neither an overly friendly letter nor a cold one, but the fact that he cared enough to write and let them know where he was made the letter a gladsome thing to his mother and sisters.

His handwriting was always remarkably neat and all the words were spelled correctly, although the punctuation and grammar usually left something to be desired. None of his uncles or aunts, David knew, had ever gotten more than a fifth-grade education. The letters were all generally the same. They usually went something like:

Dear Sister:
Just thought I would drop you a line to tell you that I have been here at Danville for the past couple of months. I have gained twelve pounds and am eating like a army mule. The weather here is good and I am off the drink and feeling fine. I hope Ma and everybody else is well. Take care of yourselves.

Your loving brother.

It was never entirely clear to David why his uncle went away so often although he knew that the departures usually followed a siege of heavy drinking and a big family fight. Mike would be on the straight and narrow for days, or sometimes for weeks, and then all of a sudden one day he would be missing when David got home from school and he wouldn't appear for a day or two. When he did finally come home he'd be drunk and ugly and mean and he'd insult his mother and sisters and do a lot of swearing, even when nobody else was in the room with him. The following morning David would hear him, very early, throwing up in the bathroom, gagging and moaning and flushing the toilet. If David saw him before going to school his uncle's clothes usually looked dirty, as if he'd slept on a sidewalk or in some alley rather than in a bed with his clothes off.

Sometimes even his Aunt Margaret would sleep with her clothes on but only when she was so tired that, lying down on the couch in the front room after dinner "just to close my eyes for a few minutes," she would not awaken until the next morning, to find that someone had removed her shoes and put a blanket over her. David could not understand how a woman her age could walk so many miles each workday, all over downtown Chicago, going into one place of business after another, to collect money for the Railway Express company.

But Mike would sleep in his clothes more often, even at home, if he had been drinking. David would find him sometimes sleeping in odd places instead of in his bed. Once he slept on the linoleum in the kitchen, another time on the floor in the front room, right next to the couch instead of on it. He had a way of wrapping one arm around under his head, so that it served as a pillow, and in that position he could sleep for hours. David had tried it once, just to see what it felt like. It felt terrible, hard and cold, and he had never made the experiment again.

When Mike was in good spirits and sober he would take David to the Lincoln Park Zoo or to the circus, if it was in town, or just for long walks in one park or another. At almost every street they crossed he'd lecture about looking both ways for traffic and as he and his nephew walked briskly along in the morning air he would advise David to take deep breaths and to keep his back straight, like a soldier. David had frequently been ill during his first years and was even now thin, which seemed to worry his uncle who consequently spoke often of men like Teddy Roosevelt and Jack Dempsey, men who knew about the importance of standing straight and drinking plenty of milk and getting plenty of fresh air and sunlight.

Mike would now and then feel the muscles on David's scrawny upper arm and pretend to marvel at its firmness. David hoped that he might one day grow to be as strong and tall as his uncle who seemed somehow indestructible although his health was obviously not perfect. On certain cold mornings as they walked his uncle would step to the curb and cough and spit up phlegm and mention his "catarrh," or he would breathe heavily and pat himself on the upper chest and say something about his "ticker," which David knew meant his heart. Bum ticker. That was what they called heart trouble. Most people who died seemed to be troubled by bum tickers or by "consumption." Grandma Considine had died of cancer but that was a strange, exotic disease that smelled bad and frightened David in a mysterious way that bum tickers and consumption did not.

But whether he was drunk or sober, in good or poor health, his Uncle Mike was invariably gentle with him, even when he had reason to be angry. David could remember the time when, moving through the long, dark hallway that ran from the living room, past the bedrooms and dining room, back to the kitchen—the hallway that had always seemed a bit frightening except when the light at its mid-point was turned on—his uncle had made a sudden noise behind the dining-room drapery and said, "Boo!"

Although he had meant to frighten David he was merely being playful, but David did not understand that. He was overcome by shock and fear and in a sudden flash of rage kicked at his uncle as hard as he could. He was only six at the time but he was wearing brand-new shoes. The point of his shoe caught Mike squarely on the right shinbone and he exhaled as he felt the pain. But the remarkable thing was that he did not get angry at David. He held him at arm's length for a moment till the boy calmed down and then he laughed a little and said, "I'm sorry, old-timer. I didn't mean to give you that bad a scare."

He carried the scar on his shin from that day.

Another reason David loved Mike was his sense of humor. His uncle did not tell jokes or funny stories and he wasn't the life-of-the-party type, but in ordinary conversation he seemed to be able to perceive and isolate the humorous element. Then too he had a few little meaningless phrases that he used to share with David, who always laughed at them even though he never knew what they meant.

"Do you know Tap Max?" Mike might say when he was just slightly drunk.

"Who's that?" David would demand, playing the game, pretending mock seriousness.

"He's a friend of Calingo Red's."

"Who's Calingo Red?"

"He works with Tap Max."

The Wake

Once in a while Mike would say something about Calingo
Red or Tap Max being in the Rocky Mountains or working
on some railroad or other, but David never had found out
who they were, although he had the clear impression that
they did exist. Mike used to talk a great deal about railroads
and traveling on freight cars and cabooses. No doubt he considered himself a railroad man, despite the infrequency of
his employment. He dressed like a railroad man, usually wearing blue work shirts and old cheap dark blue suits. He rolled
his own cigarettes with Bull Durham tobacco and would give
the little cloth bags to David, to keep marbles or pennies in.
In his back pocket he always carried a large dark blue
handkerchief with white dots.

David loved to hear him talk of the Rocky Mountains and
the oil fields and farms and army life and flophouses and
strange places he had visited. The one place that David
guessed his uncle had never traveled to was the deep South.
And that was odd because when he got drunk he would
sometimes speak with a southern accent. Not when he was
angry, but when he was trying to amuse David.

He remembered now the time his uncle had come home
drunk and wild, when they all were living in another apartment. He had broken some dishes in the kitchen and chased
his mother and sisters to bed and told them all to go to hell.
So David and the women did go to bed, leaving Mike roaming
around the house, muttering to himself, cursing and bump-
ing into things.

At the time David had shared a bedroom with his Aunt
Margaret, a room with a very small porch off it, which could

be entered by a door from the living room. After he had lain in the darkness for perhaps an hour, whispering to his aunt, a rainstorm had suddenly come up, having threatened throughout the day. David lay quietly for a while, listening to the thunder, watching patterns flashing across the walls and ceiling from the lights of cars that swished by in the rain.

Suddenly they both heard the door to the front porch open.

"My God," his aunt said, "he's going out there in the rain."

Sure enough, Mike walked out onto the small porch, mumbling to himself. David could see him clearly, as a flash of lightning washed the scene white. Then he laughed because he could see that his uncle had come home with a peculiar haircut, with the hair much too short, like a convict's. He was standing out on the porch in his long underwear, looking like Slim Summerville in a comedy movie David had seen only a few weeks earlier.

"Oh, God, no," Margaret said. "I hope he doesn't try to sit in that chair."

There was an old-fashioned beach chair, wooden, with yellow and green striped canvas, and David knew if his uncle tried to use it he would have trouble. It was a cheap chair and you had to lower yourself into it very gingerly or it would collapse, partially or completely. David was not surprised when he heard the sound of the chair being pulled and knocked about and his uncle swearing.

"Is he going to sleep out there in the rain?" he asked his aunt, giggling at the prospect.

"Hush up," she said. "If he hears you laughing he'll keep

up that foolishness all night long, if it doesn't make him mad."

The wind began to blow more violently and David heard his uncle say in a loud voice, "Blow, you son of a bitch, blow!"

The wind obliged and by the next flash of lightning they could see that Mike was drenched to the skin. As he turned Margaret could see that he was not wearing his false teeth. He looked like a wild Indian.

"My God," Margaret said, "if anybody sees him out there like that we'll get arrested."

A minute or two later the wind and rain lightened and then abruptly stopped altogether. There was no sound except the drip and trickle of water from drainpipes and eaves. Then, from somewhere to the right, they could hear the steady click-click of a man's hard leather heels coming closer along the sidewalk that ran right below the porch. When Margaret heard the footsteps she said, "Jesus, Mary and Joseph."

Then, in the momentary stillness, over the gurgle of the running water, as the heel sounds passed below, David heard his uncle say, "Say, brothah . . ."

From the street below came a startled "What?"

"Pahdon me, podnuh," said Mike, speaking with the mellow accents of the South, "but ah was wonderin' if pe'haps you maght have a cigarette."

David got a fit of giggling so bad that his aunt had to press her hand over his mouth. Shortly thereafter he fell asleep happy.

He called now through the screen door. "Uncle Mike! Come on in."

Mike came in, saying, "What's the matter, old-timer?"

"Nothing," David said. "Mama thought you'd all be warmer in here."

"Did she now?" Mike said. He went to the sink and began to wash a few dishes and pans. Josie came in fast, blowing her nose, her eyes red and wild.

"Oh, God, Mike," she said. "Why did she have to die?"

"Well, Christ, Josie, she *was* eighty-six years old. I think that had somethin' to do with it."

"Oh, sure," she said, "I know *you* don't care."

"What do you mean, I don't care? I care as much as any of you. It's just that I don't go around asking a lot of stupid questions like why did she have to die."

"Ah, you!" she said, stomping out.

"What are you doing, Uncle Mike?" David said.

"Washing some pots and pans, Davey. You want to give me a hand?"

"Sure."

"Okay, get that dish towel and dry this." He handed the boy a wet frying pan.

"What do you want me to do with it when I'm finished drying it, Uncle Mike?"

With his right hand David was playing with the yo-yo.

"Just hang it there on the hook over the stove."

"Okay."

His uncle continued washing pots and pans, whistling "Sunbonnet Sue" softly. David finished drying the pan but instead of hanging it up as instructed he placed it on a burner and went on playing with his yo-yo. After a moment he remembered that he had not completed his task and with his left hand picked up the pan. Instead of settling properly on its hook the pan slipped from his fingers and fell to the stove with a shocking clatter.

Mike whirled, instantly frightened and furious, and slapped the yo-yo from David's hand.

"Goddamn it!" he said, and then looked stricken. "Oh, pardon my French, old-timer," he said, bending to retrieve the yo-yo. "I didn't mean to slap you like that. I guess my nerves are all shot."

"I'm sorry, Uncle Mike," David said. "I didn't mean to drop it."

"That's okay, pardner," Mike said. "I always was a little too quick with my dukes, I guess. My mind was a million miles away and the noise gave me a scare."

Jack entered from the porch.

"What's wrong?" he said. "What happened?"

"Nothin', Goddamn it," Mike said, then winced again. "I'm *sorry*, Davey," he said.

"Sorry about what?" Belle said, coming from the hall.

"Nothin', Belle," Mike said, gritting his teeth. "Davey just dropped his yo-yo."

"Crazy as a bedbug," Belle said, as if to herself.

"Who is?" Mike said.

"Not you. That Josie. She's crazy as a bedbug. She never did have too much sense, but now I think she's gone off altogether. You know what she's in there now tryin' to tell Maggie and me?"

"What?"

"That Ma's not dead. She keeps runnin' up to the coffin and sayin' 'No, no, Ma. You're not dead. You're not dead.'"

"Well," Jack said, "I guess she only means she doesn't *want* her to be dead."

"No," Belle said. "I think she actually means just what she's sayin'. She just came runnin' up to Maggie and me and she says the same thing. 'Ma's not dead. Ma's not dead.'"

"Well, Jesus," Mike said, clenching his fists. "She'd better be or I'm gonna jump right out this window. And keep on goin'."

Margaret came in and said, "Belle, will you leave poor Josie alone? Davey, why don't you go out and play?"

"Will I leave *her* alone?" Belle snapped. "Listen, I gave her the air years ago. Don't give me any abuse about that one. Whatever bee she's got in her bonnet right now *I* had nothin' to do with putting it there! David, didn't you hear your Aunt Mag? Go on out and play!"

Alarmed by the anger of the adults, David walked out to the back yard.

"What's the matter, sister?" Jack said, quietly.

"Don't ask me!" Belle said. "I'm on my good behavior, and you know it, Maggie."

"All right, Belle," Margaret said. "Then I'm sorry. I thought it was something you said that set poor Josie off." She walked back to the parlor.

"Poor Josie," Belle muttered sarcastically. Suddenly she felt uneasy under Jack's gaze.

"Would you like a cup of coffee, Belle?" he said.

"What? Oh, no thanks. How come you're so nice all of a sudden? Ah, yeah, I forgot; you want to pester me about Davey."

"No," he said, "I just wanted to ask you if you've thought about what you're going to do with him."

"Yes, I have, and it's settled!"

"Then Davey was right. You're taking him with you?"

"I'm not taking him anyplace," she snapped. "He stays here, with Maggie!"

"But you can't do that to him, Belle, he—"

"Do what to him? Listen, I—"

"I'm sorry," he said. "My only concern is for Davey."

"So is mine. Who do you think pays for his room, his board, everything he needs? Me! And where do I *get* the money? I work Goddamn hard for it. I'm not complaining. The money's good. But here's the laugh; you all want me to give it up. For what? To go back to a 'respectable' job, in the shoe factory or someplace, at twenty-five a week? You're all nuts! I ain't gonna do it! As long as I can make the kinda money I make, Maggie will get her check in the mail every month."

"Belle," Jack said, wishing he could hold it back, "how do you put your *love* in an envelope and mail it to a little boy?"

Stung, she rushed to the attack. "Have you been drinkin'?"

"A little," he said. "Maybe I wouldn't have the courage to talk like this if I hadn't. Maybe the reason we Irish drink is that with a couple of shots in us we can say things that otherwise might stay bottled up."

"Well, listen," she said, "you're tryin' the wrong psychology if you think you can make me feel guilty about the—"

"Psychology," he shouted, spitting the word back at her. "God, do you even know what the word *means?* Listen, Belle, no matter how much we explore the human mind we don't ever seem able to reach the horizon. But there are a *few* things we know. And one of them is that a lot of the problems that people face as adults, the terrible things that make them *hateful* to each other, were caused by awful things that happened to them when they were just little children."

"So what?"

"Christ," he said, "can't you see what you're doing to that *boy?*"

She wanted to run from the room to evade his ruthless prosecution but felt she must somehow justify herself.

"Listen," she said, "somebody must have done something to *us* as kids, too, to make us what we are."

"Passin' the buck back to Ma and the old man, eh? Well, it won't work. You didn't come from a broken home."

"The hell I didn't!"

"No," he pressed on, "the old man didn't leave us till we were all practically grown up. *You* left before *he* did, to go with the circus."

"Listen, we *all* had to go to *work,* didn't we? When you're poor you don't have the—"

"Don't hand me that," he said. "If we were poor we were still better off than millions of others. And we were raised in the Church." He paused for a moment and looked at the steam on the cold window, over the teakettle. "No, whatever makes *us* so wild is more of a mystery. It's just there, like the color of our eyes and hair. I don't think our *childhood* has that much to do with it. Sometimes, I swear to God, I think we Irish are a bunch of *savages* with just a thin veneer of Christianity painted over us."

"Good God," she said, "I don't know why you're always knockin' your own people. The Irish have got more charm than all the rest of them put together."

"Sure," he laughed bitterly, "they *have* to. We could never get away carrying that much anger around in our hearts if we hadn't learned to wear a smilin' face."

For a reason he could not understand he was even angrier now, rebelling against something.

"The Irish," he said, mimicking her boastful tone, "you think that because we're Irish that makes us the center of the universe, some sort of yardstick that every other nationality or race or religion has to measure up to?"

"What in the name of God are you talking about?"

"Ah, hell," he said, turning away. "Never mind. I still think it's your *duty* to make a home for Davey."

"Shut up!" she shouted. "I've had *enough* of your advice. With a vicious tongue like that it's no *wonder* you got kicked out of the seminary. My God, nothin' has changed around this house. I always got the blame for everything and it looks like I always will."

He shrugged helplessly as she stomped from the room. At that inopportune moment the front door opened and a woman in her late thirties stepped tentatively into the vestibule, followed by a scowling, square-jawed boy of ten and a pretty blond girl somewhat younger.

"Hello?" she called. "The door was open."

Chuck McDermott, having observed that no member of the family had responded to the first knocking, had risen and started for the door. The woman he now met had a pleasant face, dark-red hair and a sealskin coat.

"Hello," she said to Chuck, whom she could not recall having ever met, "I'm Nellie Riley. The door was open."

"That's fine," Chuck said. "Come in. Oh, here's Belle."

"My God," Belle cried, her face still flushed with anger, but now smiling at the sight of an old friend. "Nellie! How are ya?"

"Belle," the visitor said, as they embraced, "it's wonderful to see you. I'm only sorry it had to be at a time like this."

"My God, Nell, how've you been?"

"Just fine, Belle. You're looking well."

"Oh, I should have had my hair marcelled yesterday, but I'll live. Don't tell me these are your kids?"

"Yes, Belle. This is Frank, Junior, and this is Theresa." The children nodded and smiled.

"They're so big," Belle said. "The boy is the picture of Frank."

"Yes, he is. Well, Belle, we were awful sorry to hear about poor Bridget, God bless her."

"I was pretty damned sorry to hear about it myself," Belle said bitterly.

"Has there been any trouble?"

"Ha! A better question would be—has there been any peace? That's all there is in this house is trouble."

"Ah, that's too bad. Francis, Theresa, go over and say a prayer for the repose of poor Mrs. Scanlan's soul." The boy and his sister went to the coffin, knelt and began to pray.

"What happened?" Nellie said.

"Well, I called the house to tell Maggie I'd be home to see Ma, and she says to me, 'You can't come home.' And I says, 'What do you mean, I can't come into my own mother's house?' And she says, 'It's on account of Josie's here,' and when I heard that I was wild! 'Oh, sure,' I said. 'I've been doing plenty of shelling out. *That* was okay, wasn't it?' Well, Nellie, I tell ya, I hadn't had a drink in ages, but when I heard that I got off the wagon and fast!"

"Ah, that's too bad, Belle."

"Too bad, hell. Anyway, I'm here now, and so far there hasn't been a blowup, but I know it's coming because that Josie won't let me alone. But this time if I go, just to spite Maggie and the boys, I'm gonna drag Davey with me!"

"How is he, Belle?"

"Oh, he's fine. I mean his health's all right, I guess. He's stubborn, just like his father's side, but he's a good boy."

The visitor began to remove her black kid gloves. "How can you take him with you on the road, Belle?"

"God, I don't know. But I can't leave him *here* forever. Each time I come back it seems he's grown a little farther away from me. I'm sure somebody here is turning him against me. God knows what they tell him about me when I'm away."

"Oh, go on," Nellie Riley said in a mollifying tone, "the boy must love you very much. But listen, I just happened to think of something. I mean, if you ever absolutely *have* to get him out of here, and you can't keep him yourself, I'd be glad to take him in. After all, I've got these two and three more at home. One extra wouldn't mean a thing."

"Well, that's very good of you, Nellie. But I wouldn't want to impose."

"Believe me, Belle, it'd be no trouble at all. And what are old friends for if you can't count on 'em when you're in a spot? Listen, let me take a look at your poor mother and then I could stand a good hot cup of tea." She excused herself and walked into the parlor.

"Fine," Belle called. "I'll go make sure there's hot water."

The boy rose from the padded kneeler and signaled his sister.

"Come on, Theresa," he said. "Let's go outside."

"Mama, can we go outside for a little while?" the girl whispered.

"All right," her mother said, "but not for long. And behave."

Outside the children met David, who was spinning a yo-yo.

"Hi," he said. "You guys at my grandma's wake?"

"Yeah," the boy said. "Who are *you?*"

"David Considine."

"I'm Theresa Riley. This is my brother Frank. I think our mom is a friend of yours. Of your mom's, I mean."

"Oh, yeah?"

"Let's see the yo-yo," Frank said.

"Okay," David said. He handed the bright blue speckled Duncan yo-yo to the larger boy, who played with it briefly.

"It's not a very good one," he said at last.

"It is too," David said. "My Uncle Jack gave it to me."

"I don't care who gave it to ya," the boy said. "It ain't no good."

"Give it back then."

"In a minute." He flipped the yo-yo down again, deftly.

"Frank!" his sister said. "Give it back."

"Aw, shut up," he said.

"I will not."

"Come on," David said, uneasy because of the larger boy's attitude. "Please."

"Say *pretty* please," the boy said contemptuously.

"Frank, don't be such a bully," Theresa said.

"Shut up."

"Well, you don't always have to act so rotten."

"I'll act anyway I like," the boy said.

"Gimme my yo-yo," David said.

Frank said, mimicking David, "Gimme my yo-yo."

"Come on," David said, "give it back or I'll tell my mom."

"Oh, yeah?"

"Yeah," David said. Then he called toward the house, "Oh, Mama Belle."

"Okay, mama's boy. Here." The visitor returned the yo-yo.

"Who wants your stupid yo-yo?" he said. In the next moment he swung a false punch at David, who drew back in alarm.

"Yah, ha!" the older boy cried. "You flinched! That means you got one coming."

"Okay," David said. He turned his shoulder to Frank, Jr., who punched him stiffly.

"Frank!" Theresa said. "You didn't have to hit him so hard."

"Ah, dry up!" There was a pause.

"How old was your grandma?" Theresa asked, smiling.

"I don't know," David said. "Eighty something, I think."

"Did you cry?" Theresa asked.

"When?"

"When she died."

"I don't know," David said. "I guess so." He whistled a minor-key melody.

"Do you know that song?" Theresa said.

"What song?"

"The one you're whistling. 'The Worms Crawl In, the Worms Crawl Out.'"

"Yeah." They began to sing softly:

> "Do you ever think
> When the hearse goes by
> That you may be
> The next to die?
>
> They wrap you up
> In a dirty shirt
> And cover you over
> With gravel and dirt.

> The worms crawl in
> And the worms crawl out
> They crawl in your belly
> And all about . . ."

Theresa and David laughed heartily.

"Hey," Frank said, "did you say your last name was Considine?"

"Yes," David said.

"Is *your* mom the fat drunk?"

"The what?"

"My mom said she was gonna see an old friend of hers today, Belle Considine. And I heard my dad say she was a heavy drinker."

"Frank!" Theresa cut in.

"You shut up!" David shouted. "You dirty bastard! You shut up about my mama!" He ran at the other boy who tripped him easily and threw him to the ground.

"Don't get smart, ya sissy, or there's more where that came from!"

Theresa pushed Frank back. "Frank, stop it. Leave him alone!"

"He called me a bastard!"

"Leave him alone! You don't even know what a bastard is."

"I do too! It's a dirty Protestant! Dad's always talkin' about the dirty Protestant bastards and nobody ain't gonna call *me* a Protestant!"

David, getting to his feet, ran into the house, looking for

his mother. He found her with Nellie Riley, at the dining-room table, drinking tea.

"Mama!" David said, breathlessly.

"David, ssshh—not so loud," his mother said. "What's the matter? What have you been up to?"

"Oh . . ." he paused, "nothin'."

"My God, Belle, so this is little Davey," Nellie said.

"Yes. How long has it been since you saw him, Nellie?"

"Well, he was only about two, I think, when I saw you and his father in Kansas City that time, remember?"

"Yeah. I guess you're right. That was just before Billy died."

"And he's how old now?"

"Seven."

"Eight," David said.

"Oh, that's right," his mother said. "I keep forgetting—you had a birthday last month. God, Nellie," she laughed throatily, "will you ever forget the time it was Dan Donohue's birthday and Big Tom Fogarty took us out to White City and we all got stinkin' on hard cider and you threw up in the back seat of—"

David did not want to hear any more. He walked quickly into the parlor and stood near his Aunt Margaret. The old women were softly saying the rosary.

"Are you getting hungry, honey?" his aunt asked.

"No, I don't think so."

"I can fix you a sandwich in a minute. Or maybe a nice hot bowl of soup?"

"Naw, I guess not." She put her arm about David's shoulder. They walked together into a bedroom.

"Aunt Mag," David said, sitting on the unmade bed, "how long will my mom be able to stay?"

"I don't know exactly, honey. Three or four days, I imagine. Why?"

"Is there *any* way I could go with her when she goes?"

"I don't know, Davey. I do know that we'd miss you terribly here if you left. And you do have to go to school somewhere, you know."

"Yeah, I guess so." He stared glumly at the floor, feeling suddenly strangely cold in his chest.

"I can't see any way that you could go with your mother and go to school, too. Of course, when summertime comes, well, that's another matter."

"Then why couldn't I go with her last summer?"

"Well, I—she was very busy, honey. You know, breaking in a new act, I think it was. But we had fun here, didn't we? Going to White City and Lincoln Park and Riverview. And I got you those new roller skates you wanted. And you got to spend two weeks with Grandma Considine. I thought it was a real nice summer."

"Oh, yeah. We did *some* things that were fun."

"Would you like me to move to another neighborhood, honey? Maybe farther east near the lake. I know there are some pretty tough kids around here. Maybe you'd be happier if you went to some other school than St. Ambrose."

"I don't know. School's all right, I guess."

"I'll tell you what. You go on out to the kitchen, or sit

here and do your homework. I'll talk to your mother and see if she has any helpful ideas. Okay?"

"Okay." David strolled toward the kitchen area, where at that moment John O'Toole was saying, "Ya know, it's gettin' so I'm afraid to read the death notices in the *Trib*. It seems there's always somebody I know that's dyin'."

"I thought you spent all your time readin' the help-wanted ads, John," Jack said, chuckling.

"Jeez, maybe they're one and the same," O'Toole said. "Maybe the death notices is a help-wanted ad run by Almighty God."

"Well, Davey-boy, how's it goin'?" Jack greeted him. "My goodness, but you're growin' up to be a fine young man."

"You do remember your Uncle Jack, don't you, Dave?"

"I guess so," David said.

"Only from pictures, I guess," Jack said. "He was only as big as that—" he gestured with his hand, "when I was here last. Davey-boy, we were just talkin' about the meaning of life. What does the catechism tell you as to why we're alive at all?"

"We are born to know God, to love him and serve him in this life, and be happy with him forever in the next," David recited.

"Good boy," Jack said. "If only a man could keep his eye on the pages of the catechism and never have to look up at life around him, as it's really lived."

"Ah, what does it all mean?" Mike said. "We're always complainin' that life is too short, and yet we all go runnin' through it as fast as we can. When we're babies we want to go to school, and once we're in school we can't wait to get out, and when we're out we can't wait to grow up, and when you grow up we can't wait to—to what? To make a nest egg, I guess. To win a couple of ball games, somehow. Or maybe just to settle for gettin' a decent job. And then when we get the job we can't wait to retire. What is it, I wonder, that we can't wait to do after we retire?"

"It can't be just to die, can it?" Jack said.

"God, I hope not," Mike said.

"I sometimes think, Mike," Jack continued, "that the main reason we believe in an afterlife is that this one is so much less than it's cracked up to be. This *can't* be all there is to it. It can't! We start out the game as dumb as a calf in a stable, and by the time we get it all figured out, by the time we finally get the idea how to play the game, it gets dark out and the game is over."

Seated at the unlovely Montgomery Ward table in the dining room, Belle said, "Was her health bad the last few weeks, Mag?"

"Not really," her sister said. "Oh, you know, she was always tired and all but until just the last few days she seemed fine."

"You know what I was just rememberin'?" Belle said.

"What?"

"How when we were all little we used to love to sit on the floor next to her rockin' chair and have her rub our heads."

"She was a wonderful mother to all of you," Nellie Riley said.

"Yes," Belle said, "but that's the nicest memory of all, for me. The way her fingers used to slip through our hair, so soft. I never felt so peaceful in my life as I did at those times."

"It sorta made up for Dada," Margaret said.

"Well, now I'm sure your father loved yez all too," Nellie said.

"Oh, yeah, but he didn't show it the way Ma did. He was so busy puttin' the fear o' God into our hearts that he didn't have much time left for anything else, I guess," Belle said, then she laughed.

"God, Mag," she said, "do you remember how we all used to look out the window when he came home to see what kind of a look he had on his face. If he looked mean we all laid low for fear he'd kill us."

"Well," Mag said, "Ma was so soft on us all, and somebody had to lay down the law."

"I guess so," Belle said. "Well, he was good to *me*."

"That he was, Belle," her sister said. "I think he thought you were the most like him, in some ways."

"How do you mean?" Nellie asked.

"Oh, I don't know. He had a certain glint in his eye, a certain devilment, sometimes, where you couldn't tell if he was about to laugh or about to kill ya, or both."

"I know what you mean," Belle said. "He did have a great sense of humor. God, how he loved to laugh. I remember he used to ask us all to read the papers to him—he never learned to read in the old country, ya know, Nell—and I was the only one who'd do it. Mag would have but I guess she was already workin' by then. Anyway, he'd sit in his easy chair in the evenin' and I'd sit on the floor at his feet and read him the papers, sometimes for hours. When I'd read about some terrible murder or somethin' like that he'd say, 'Glory be to God, what's this country comin' to?' And when I'd read some funny story sometimes he'd get a fit o' laughin' where I thought he'd never stop. It's funny, he would never laugh with Ma. He loved her and all, but she didn't have his sense of humor."

"That's what I was just sayin', Belle," her sister said. "You were his favorite because he loved to laugh. And God knows he had little reason to around this house."

"Ya know," Nellie said, "I don't remember your father all that well, it's been so many years ago, but we have a picture of him at our house and it seems to me little Davey is the image of him."

"I can see what you mean," Margaret said. "Around the eyes. That funny look like half a frown and half a smile."

"Ah, God, Maggie," Belle sighed. "I don't know what I'm gonna do with him."

"He talks about you all the time, Belle," Margaret said. "He loves you so much."

"Well, don't sound so damned disappointed about it. He's *supposed* to love his mother, isn't he? Although it's a wonder he still does. God knows what you all tell him about me when I'm not around."

"I don't mean to butt in, to something that's not my business," Nellie Riley said, "but I know that nobody is talking against you here. Certainly not to your own child, Belle."

"Well, I hope you're right, Nell. But I wouldn't put it past them. And if Maggie or Rose or Mike wouldn't do it, I wouldn't put it past Josie."

"She's only *been* here for a few days, Belle," Margaret said. "You know that."

"All it takes is a few minutes," Belle said bitterly.

"Are you sayin' that the love that that child has for you could be swept out of his heart with just a few words of criticism?" Margaret said.

"Oh, I don't know. But the way you're all acting you'd think I was some sort of a monster who didn't *want* the boy with me on the road. What do you think it makes me feel like when I see other mothers with their children? Playing on their lawns and going to their churches and carrying them in their arms and whatever. Do you think that a day passes that isn't filled with heartbreak for me?"

"Maggie knows that, Belle," Nellie said. "She's just trying to be helpful."

"Well," Belle said, "I know what this family thinks of me being in show business. And, to tell the truth, there are times when I can see their point. Here at home I'm no different from the rest of ya. But a woman in show business has to think of herself first, last and always. There's no other way. Not because we want to, for God's sake. It just works out that way. To keep ourselves alive we have to tell people what to do, we have to give the orders. We have to tell agents what to do, tell managers what to do, tell straight men and musicians and stagehands and bellboys what to do. So, sure, we wear the pants. What the hell are we supposed to do? Let people walk all over us? No, we *have* to wear the pants. The only thing is that, as we get older, it begins to show. When you're young and pretty they'll take it, and maybe even think it's cute. But when you start headin' over the hill, then they call you hard and bossy and masculine."

"Ah, come on, Belle," Nellie said, "don't be feelin' so sorry for yourself. You've got your health and you're makin' good money and you've got a child who idolizes you."

David had drifted into the hallway. He now stood listening to the women, unnoticed by them.

"Ah, God," Belle said, "I never should have *had* him. I guess I'm not the mother type. I love him and all, but—I don't know—I can't give up show business. Not even for him. I couldn't stand to live back here in Chicago again. There's too much sadness here for me. Nothing could make me go back to it. And how the hell would I live, anyway? I've had to support myself from the time I was ten years old. You know that, Maggie. Ma farmed me out to the Watson Sisters in the circus and for three years I lived like a slave. But I lived. I didn't take a penny from Ma or any of the boys. And *you* remember, Maggie, what it was like workin' in the shoe factory. Long hours, lousy money. People gettin' fingers and hands chopped off. Five years of sheer hell. What am I supposed to do, go back to that? And what do I know *how* to do? Nothin' but give people a song and a dance. How can you ask me to give that up? It's the only thing that's ever brought me any kind of happiness at all." Her eyes filled with tears.

"Nobody's asking you to give it up, Belle," her sister said.

Standing in the darkness of the hallway, David was afraid to breathe, afraid to move. He looked at his hands in an odd way, as if to see if he was still visible, even to himself.

"No, but how you all love to make me feel guilty about Davey! How did I know his father was going to die and leave me flat broke and stranded? How did I know I was going to have a child in the first place. After three miscarriages! Well, never mind. Now that I'm *stuck* with him I'll call the turn. Don't you worry about that."

The cold feeling in David's chest was now so severe that he shivered. In a stunned fury he ran down the hall and into a bedroom, slamming the door behind him.

CHAPTER FIVE

Jack waited until he had another opportunity to speak to Belle alone. It came when he offered to help dry the dishes after she had washed a few coffee cups and saucers.

"Listen," he said, "I've been thinkin' about Davey and I did have one idea, but then I decided it was no good."

"What was it?" she said.

"Well, I was thinkin' he might like to come stay with me for a while in Boston. But I guess he doesn't know me that well, and anyway the best solution would be to find some way he could stay with you."

"No matter what I do with him, it'll give somebody around here somethin' to complain about," she said.

"Well, that's not the point, Belle," he said. "We're not interested in criticizing you for what you do."

"Oh, no?"

"No, I'm just tryin' to be helpful is all."

"Well, so far the best idea seems to be just to leave him here, with Maggie."

"I'm not sure that's the best arrangement now that Ma's dead."

"Well, who the hell *asked* you?"

"Let me finish," he said, working hard to keep his voice down. "We both know that Mag loves him and takes great care of him. But he needs his mother."

"You know damn well I can't take him on the road," she said, springing up from the table.

"All right then. Have you ever thought about settling down? Making a home for the both of you?"

"Yeah," she said sarcastically, "that'd be nice all right. How would I *eat?*"

"With a knife and fork, like the rest of us."

"Damn it, Jack, I'm serious," she said, beginning to pace. "Can't you see I'm trapped? The kid has to stay put in one place and get his schooling. And I can't settle down."

"Aw, God," he said, sighing. "How do other actors raise their kids?"

"Like I do, I guess. Put 'em in boarding schools, farm them out to relatives. I don't know, and I don't care. I only know about me, Belle Considine!"

"Belle," Jack said slowly, "I was hoping you wouldn't force me to play this card. I happen to know that Billy Considine's mother offered to pay for room and board for you and Davey when his father died, if you'd just make a home for him!"

Stunned, she turned away from his gaze. "I don't accept charity from anyone!"

"All right, then let me ask you something I maybe shouldn't ask. Ah, to hell with it. Why don't you *marry* Doug Roberts and let *him* support the both of you?"

"You're Goddamn right you shouldn't ask!" she shouted,

out of control now. "But since you did I'll tell you. He hasn't *asked* me."

"I'm sorry," Jack said, and for the moment gave up.

Later that night, in the kitchen, John O'Toole was playing the harmonica, though not very well, in a six-eight Irish jig tempo. While the rest of the men looked on and laughed, Tommy Monaghan did a clumsy little dance and sang:

> "Oh, her mother's name was Cleo
> and her father's name was Pat,
> so they called her Cleopatra;
> Now whadda ya think of that?"

Tommy did a comedy bow and the others gave him mock applause.

"Say," Matty Mulcahey said, "has anybody got enough for a fresh bottle?"

"No," Chuck McDermott said, "I'm a little short," bending his knees to look shorter. "Jeez, Matty," he added, "that reminds me of the time down in Bughouse Square when a well-dressed character gets up and says, "I just lost my wallet with five hundred dollars in it, and I'll give fifty bucks to the man that finds it. And Tommy here yells, 'I'll give seventy-five!'"

They all laughed and smiled at each other.

"Well," Matty said, "if we ain't got enough to pay for another pint, can somebody let me have a *cigarette*, for Christ's sake?"

"Matty," Tommy said, "I thought you was *off* the cigarettes."

"Well, I was, for about a month."

"Sure," Chuck said, "he had the lumbago for a month and couldn't bend over and pick 'em up!"

"Go wan, ya crazy bastard," Matty said good-naturedly.

"Listen, Matty," Mike said, "if you're desperate for another belt, I can let you have a little of what I've got left here."

"No, that's all right, Mike," Matty said, "forget it."

"Don't tell me you're turnin' down a drink, Matty," Chuck said.

"Well, I am."

"Go on," Chuck said, appealing to the others, "the only time *he* ever turned his back on a drink was the time he drove a brewery truck."

"That's not true," big John O'Toole said, with mock solemnity. "He was on the wagon once. It was the worst fifteen minutes he ever spent in his life."

"Chuck, sing us another song," Jack said, draining his glass.

"Damned if I won't. Professor, a little waltz clog, please."

He rose and did a little waltz clog as he sang, accompanied by O'Toole's harmonica:

> "Sure, me name is Cornelius Maguire
> And I come clear from Cleveland, Ohi-er.
> If you're wonderin' why
>   There is smoke in me eye,
> Well, my *pipe* set me *britches* on fire!"

They all laughed and applauded louder then ever.

"You know who used to know a lotta funny songs," O'Toole said, "was poor old Jimmy McManus."

"God rest his soul," Matty Mulcahey added.

"I didn't know he passed away," Chuck said. "How did he die?"

"He died in his bed," Mike said, "of a perfectly natural case of delirium tremens."

"McManus. He was the *boxer*, wasn't he?" Jack asked.

"That's right," Chuck said, "he worked one time, ya know, as a sparring partner for Jack Dempsey."

"For how long?" Jack said.

"About two rounds."

"God," O'Toole said wistfully, "that Dempsey had a wicked right, didn't he?" He threw a couple of right jabs, playing, dancing around Chuck McDermott. "He musta had a lotta Irish blood."

"Yeah," McDermott said, "when he fought McManus he had *Jimmy's* blood all over him." O'Toole and Chuck continued to spar.

"Had enough?" Chuck said, after quickly getting the worst of it.

"Who do ya think was the better man," he asked Jack, "*Dempsey* or *Gene Tunney?*"

"They were both terrific," Jack said, "but I always thought Jack Johnson coulda killed the two o' them at the same time."

O'Toole whirled and faced Jack angrily, in a fighting pose. "What the hell are you *talkin'* about, Jack? No *nigger* could ever have beat Jack Dempsey!" Momentarily shocked by

O'Toole's narrow-mindedness, Jack looked up quickly, but merely shrugged.

"That's one way to look at it," he said.

"Ah, I don't know, boys," Matty Mulcahey, the peacemaker, said. "Wakes don't seem to be as much *fun* as they used ta."

"That's true," Tommy Monaghan agreed. There was another pause.

"Yes, sir," Jack said.

They paused again.

"Yessirree, sir," O'Toole said, inspecting his hands.

"Oh, Lordy, Lordy, Lordy, Lordy, Lordy," Mike whispered in one softly exhaled breath.

"Let's have that bottle again," Jack said.

Mike lifted an unlabeled pint bottle from his coat pocket, took a drink from it, wiped off the mouth of the bottle and passed it to Jack, who drank, making a wry face.

"Bah!" he said. "They call that whiskey? Tastes more like battery acid."

O'Toole reached for the bottle and lifted it as a "toast." "To your dear mother, fellas," he said. "May she rest in peace." He drank deeply.

"Listen, John," Jack said sarcastically, "another belt of that stuff and you'll rest in peace yourself."

"Yeah," Mike said. "I thought you were goin' on the wagon."

"I thought I was meself," O'Toole recalled. "Bah," he said, "I've tasted canned *heat* that was better than this stuff. God, what is it made of?"

"Right off the boat," Mike said, laughing.

"Yeah, *scraped* off," O'Toole said.

"Ah," Matty said, "I hope to God we all don't go blind from it."

"Well," Mike said, "when all is said and done, I suppose we'll pay for our sins one way or the other."

"Ahh, that's the trouble with us," Jack said, annoyed.

"What is?" Monaghan said after a long pause.

"Oh, the Irish like to talk about themselves, and that's the God's truth. And it all depends on our mood as to whether we decide we're devils or saints. But we make one big mistake." Jack paused sleepily.

"Well?" Mike said.

"Well, what?"

"What the hell *is* it, for Chrissake?"

"What the hell is *what*?" Jack said, trying to clear his head.

"Jeez, I don't know," Mike said. "You was sayin' we make one big mistake."

"Oh, yes," Jack said. "All right, I'll tell you what it is." But he started to doze off again.

"No, *I'll* tell you what it is," Mike said. "It's that we get so Goddamned drunk we forget what we're talkin' about."

"No," Jack said, looking up, "it's this. When we see something in ourselves that we *like*, we always attribute it to our bein' Irish—when the real roots of our virtue lie in our *humanity*—not in our Irishness. And if we don't give ourselves gold medals just for bein' Irish—which none of us could *help*, God knows—then it's for bein' Catholic. And damned few of us ever made an actual decision to be that either."

"I'm not sure I follow ya," O'Toole said.

"I'll buy that," Jack said. "Jeez, I'm fallin' asleep. I could do with some coffee." He rose and lighted the gas flame under the gray tin coffee pot on the stove. "A good shot o' java'll wake us all up."

"Right!" Mike said. "Give us another song, John."

O'Toole played mournfully on the harmonica.

"The old songs are so much better," Monaghan said, "don't you think—than the trash we've been hearin' the last few years."

"Trash?" O'Toole said.

"Yeah. Like 'Vo-do-dee-oh-do' and . . . and 'Just a Gigolo.' Jeez, what kind of a song is *that* for a real man to be singin'?"

"Right," O'Toole said, "and 'When the Midnight Choo-Choo Leaves for Alabam'.' *I* hopped a midnight choo-choo once, and wound up in Alabam', and got my butt kicked from one end of the Birmingham yards to the other. You can *have* the Southerners, as far as I'm concerned." Thinking back, he said quietly, "The dirty bastards. And I hadn't eaten a bite in two days. Give me a good *old* song, anytime. A song that means something."

"Yeah," Jack said sarcastically. "Like 'Ta-ra-ra-boom-dee-e.' There's a song that tells a beautiful story. And 'Mumbo Jumbo Jijjiboo J. O'Shea.' No, John, the trash we have always with us. Perhaps we need an eleventh commandment: Thou Shalt Produce No Trash."

A cot had been made up in the dining room for David,

who had gotten into pajamas, robe and slippers. "But I don't feel sleepy at all," he protested.

"Never mind," his mother said. "It's way past your bedtime as it is. Aunt Maggie put up the extra cot for you out here because Uncle Jack'll be using one bed and Aunt Josie'll be in the front bedroom."

Margaret entered from a bedroom. "Here's the blanket, Belle. I don't know *where* that extra pillow is."

Belle took the blanket and flung it on the cot, tucking it in.

"Where will *you* sleep?" David said.

"I don't know," Belle said. "I'll manage. Maybe on the couch."

"In with Grandma, by the coffin?"

"Yes. Although we can't put the in-a-door bed down 'cause there's no room."

"But there are people in there," David said.

"They won't stay all night."

"Belle," Margaret said, helping her with the blanket, "you can sleep in my room. Let *me* sleep on the couch."

"With Josie? I wouldn't share a bed with her. And besides, you need your rest more than I do. You have to work tomorrow."

"I don't mind."

"No," Belle said. "I'll manage. I've spent so many years sitting up all night in drafty railroad stations that just being in Ma's house again is like Heaven."

"You won't leave, will you, Mama?" David said. "When I fall asleep, I mean."

"No, honey, I won't." She felt angry and trapped.

"But the last time you did," he said. "The last time I woke up in the morning and looked over on the other side of the bed . . . and you were gone."

"Well," his mother said, "you know how we all are about saying good-by around here. We don't like good-bys."

"Then why don't you all *stay*," David said, raising his voice, "in one place? Why don't all of us just never say good-by again?"

Margaret blew her nose. "I'll go back for that pillow," she said.

"Jump in," Belle said, holding the blanket and sheet up. David climbed into bed.

"Don't you say your prayers?" she said.

"Oh, yeah." He got out of the bed, knelt beside it, made the sign of the cross, and prayed very quietly. Belle, furtively, looked down the hall both ways, lighted a cigarette and inhaled deeply. Suddenly a door opened and voices were raised in the darkened kitchen. Startled, she snuffed the cigarette out, hid the evidence, and waved her hand to dissipate the smoke in the air. David, having finished praying, got into bed once more.

"Are you sure this one blanket'll be warm enough for you?" his mother said.

"Yeah, I'm all right." He looked up at her eyes and mouth and hair hungrily.

"If it isn't I can put my sealskin coat over you. I guess there are no more extra blankets. The ones from Grandma's bed are at the laundry, I think."

"That's okay," David said. "Mama Belle, where did my daddy die?"

"In Atlanta, honey." She was startled by the unexpected question.

"Tell me what happened."

"What do you mean?"

"I mean everything. All about how he died. Nobody ever told me."

"Well, let's see," his mother said, speaking slowly at first, "our last week on the Orpheum Time that season was New Orleans. After that we were supposed to go to New York, I think, but we received a wire from Jake Lubin—he was head of the Loew Time—asking us to finish out Jimmy Savo's route down South. Since our top salary from Lubin was $225 —or was it $250 . . . anyway, I knew Jimmy Savo got lots more. I thought it was a good chance to get more money, so I wired New York we'd accept for $450."

"Did you get it?" David said, turning on his side, gratified that she chose to talk to him at length.

"Yes," she said, "which meant opening in Atlanta. In those days we always carried your little bed and bedding and put it out to air on a porch outside our room window. I remember we had a few days' layoff and it rained the first day and kept raining. Your bedding was soaked. Because of some damned Shriners' convention we had to give up our hotel room, and to kill time until our train left at night we just rode around for hours in a taxi, then ate in the restaurant. Your father looked sick, but I blamed it on his . . . his drinking. All actors drank in New Orleans, you know how it is. . . . So, we got on the sleeper, you and I in the lower, Billy in the upper. The next morning when the train was pulling into Atlanta, he said to me, 'Belle, give the porter a good tip. He's been so kind to me all night.' I just didn't really know how sick he was. We checked into the hotel and I had to dash out and get new bedding for you and—why, I'll never know . . . I bought myself a new cape and hat, both black . . . like mourning clothes. When I got back to the hotel I saw he was really terribly sick. So I called the desk clerk to get a doctor. He called for an ambulance and before going out the door Billy took off his Elk ring and said, 'Give this to Sweetie.' He was the one who started calling you 'Sweetie.'"

"When do I get the ring?"

"When you're twenty-one. I have it in a vault for you. Anyway, I couldn't find a nurse for you. I went to the Davis Fisher Hospital every day, but couldn't get any information. None of the nurses or doctors would even give me the time o' day. So I gave a colored orderly five dollars and asked him to call me—if he thought your daddy was getting worse. When I finally got to see him he wasn't quite in his right mind, and kept saying, 'Belle, where is Sweetie? Where is Davey?' He sure loved ya, all right."

"I wish I could remember."

"One day, to see if I could recall his memory, I started to say the lines of our act and he went through it all letter perfect, but it didn't help. Then on the fifth day, when I visited him, I asked at the desk, where was the closest Catholic church. The bird behind the desk answered, real nasty, 'We don't know anything about *Catholic* churches around here!'

On the way back to the hotel I saw a little colored girl, oh, about thirteen years, walking along and I asked her if she'd take care of you. She said, 'How much?' I said, 'How much do you want?' She said, 'Fifty cents a day, but I wants it every day.'"

"Did she take care of me?"

"Yes. When we got to the hotel there was a call for me from the colored orderly saying I better come to the hospital right away. So I dashed out and in my panic I took the wrong streetcar and went, God knows where, out of my way, ending up in some damned prairie. I got off the car and there was no corner or other streetcar near, so I kept trying to get someone to take me back to town. Finally, a young couple in a carriage gave me a lift. I told them about your father and they came right up to the hospital room with me. I didn't know it at first, but they even waited in the hall. The colored orderly was alone with Billy. Then the nurse came in. I picked Billy up in my arms. I was sitting at the top of the bed, and he died in my arms."

The front door opened and Josie came in, carrying a large bag of groceries. Margaret hurried in with a pillow.

"That you, Josie?" she called down the hall.

"Yes," Josephine said, "I noticed you were out of a few things so I stopped in to the A&P while I was out."

"Oh, thanks," Margaret said. "Rose said she'd go, but she's still taking a nap. We're just putting Davey to sleep." She took the pillow to David's cot and adjusted it comfortably under his head, then kissed him good night. "Goodnight, sweetie."

" 'Night, Aunt Maggie," David said. "Mama's telling me a story."

"I'll put this stuff in the kitchen," Josie said. In the kitchen she removed articles from the paper bag and put them where they belonged.

"There's fresh cream now for the coffee you're drinking, Jack, if you want any," she said.

"Thank you, Josie." Jack helped himself to the cream at the top of the fresh bottle of milk. "You fellows want some?" he said.

"No, thanks," Mike said.

"I milked so many cows right here in this neighborhood," O'Toole said, "when I was a boy, that I've never been able to look the stuff in the face since."

"Jeez, John," Tommy Monaghan said, "remember when all you could see from 47th Street was cows—and miles of cabbage fields and flowers?"

"Yes," O'Toole recalled, "hollyhocks as tall as giraffes grew around here then. And *sunflowers!* God!"

"Yeah," Jack said. "I remember them . . . glowing like the golden monstrance that shines at benediction."

"I wonder if they had sunflowers in the *old* country?" Tom mused. "All I ever heard my old man talk about was cabbages and potatoes."

"There's one thing I've never been able to get straight in my mind," O'Toole said. "Well—come to think of it, there's a million things I've never been able to get straight in my mind—but what I'm thinking now is this: Since the Irish are always talking about how beautiful the old country was and how great it was to live there, sure why did millions of 'em high-tail it to the good old U.S.A. as soon as they got the chance?"

"That's an easy one, John," Jack said. "Poverty and hunger. The shamrock is beautiful, my boy, but you can't eat it."

"Potatoes," Mike said. "Not enough potatoes, that was the problem. Jeez, I just happened to think of something funny. The Russians, ya know, discovered a way to make booze outta potatoes. It's a godsend the Irish never learned that trick or we would have been too blind to make the trip over." They all laughed heartily.

"I think our whole race never should have left home," Jack said after a moment.

"And why not?" Monaghan demanded.

"We lost somethin' on the way over," Jack said. "I'm not sure what it was. Maybe it was the poetry. I've been to the old country since I left Chicago. You'd like the Irish there better than the Irish of Chicago, I think. They've still got the poetry."

"Ah, who cares about writin' poetry?" Mike said.

"No, I'm not talkin' about *writing* it. I'm talking about *speaking* it. They still do over there, you see. Because they see things different somehow. They still *see* the mist on the meadow in the early morn, and the smoke floatin' up from the chimneys in the chilly country, and the sun crackin' down through the clouds and makin' the green grass dance. And because they see it, they talk about it. But something happened to the American Irish that put scales on our eyes. I'll be damned if I know what it was."

"Maybe," Mike said, "we lost the gift on the way over on the boat."

"I don't know," Jack said. "Maybe so. You know, the reason people say God-bless you when a man sneezes is because the ancients believed that at such times his soul might slip out of his body. Maybe on the way over the Irish got drunk and stood too near the rail and threw up so much from seasickness that they just scattered the soul and spirit of poetry to the four winds and the seven seas." They laughed. "But that wasn't it. No, somethin' happened to us *here*. I wish to God I knew what it was. It *wasn't* just poverty. Most of us were poorer in the old country than we've been here, as hard as times have been. Maybe it's that we were naturally rural people, who never should have moved to the civilized city at all."

"You might be on to somethin' there," Monaghan said. "We're nothin' much here in the States, God knows, but in the old country I hear tell we was kings."

"You hear tell wrong," Jack said. "I looked into our history a bit and it's nothin' to brag about, between you and me, Tommy."

"We was always great *fighters,*" O'Toole said, his face darkening.

"Depends on how you mean that," Jack said. "We're argumentative enough, that's for sure, and there've been some good Irish boxers—John L. and Jim Corbett and Fitzsimmons and a few others—but as military men we've always been a joke. Fighters who never won an important battle, much less a war. No, boys, mostly we fought against each other, which says something about our intelligence, it seems to me."

"Listen," O'Toole grumbled, "I ain't never been to the old country so I ain't no expert on that, but I do know there's been a lot of us ready to fight for the good old U.S.A."

"I'm not so sure," Jack said. "In the World War now there was probably as many of us hopin' that England would get beat by Germany as felt the other way around. And we talk today about what a great man Abraham Lincoln was when, by God, you should have seen what happened, when Uncle Sam tried to draft the Irish during the Civil War."

"What did happen?" said Mike.

"Oh, it was beautiful. We raised all sorts of hell. There were riots all over New York."

"I never heard o' them riots," O'Toole said. "I don't believe ya."

"Don't take my word for it, John," Jack said. "Look it up. About two thousand people were killed and thousands more were injured. And, as if that wasn't bad enough, we were such poor sports that we not only fought the government people, we took it out on poor defenseless Negroes."

"Now why would we do a thing like that?" Monaghan asked, honestly puzzled.

"Because we figured the only reason they were tryin' to draft us in the first place was to fight for the Negroes down South. And we did terrible things, terrible things."

"Such as?" O'Toole asked skeptically.

"Such as attacking a Negro *orphanage*, for Christ's sake,"

Jack said, angry now. "Is that something you're proud of, John?"

"Take it easy, Jack," said Monaghan. "Here we're doin' the very thing you was just sayin' we shouldn't do. Fightin' amongst ourselves."

"That's the God's truth," Chuck McDermott said.

"I'm sorry, Tom," Jack said. "You're right."

"The Irish really ought to stick together," McDermott said. "There's too many others would like to do us no favors."

"Right," Matty Mulcahey said. "One o' the big problems around Chicago is there's too much competition."

"Right," Mike said. "Too many people who'd cut your throat to get ahead o' ya."

"You may be on to somethin' there," Jack said. "In the old country the Irish had only *two* enemies . . . the English and the Protestants, and they were usually the same. But here we've had dozens of enemies."

"Christ," Mike said, "the question is—have we had any *friends?*"

"Well, if we haven't, Mike," Jack said, "it's been of our own doin'. Other people get along pretty well. Who put the chip on *our* shoulders? The thing is . . . I love the Irish, but only in our historic roles . . . as underdogs. Ah, we were marvelous under the British. Sympathetic, courageous, willing to do battle with a smile or a song on our lips. But in America success went to our heads. Look at the big, tragic joke of it. We couldn't stand the British because they were always standing over us, telling us what to do. That was their sin. So what do *we* do here? We flock like angry sheep into

The Wake

three professions—the *priesthood,* the *police* and *politics*—
and the three professions have just this in common—that they
entitle us to stand over others, to give *others* the orders.

"Don't tell me about our dedication to freedom, boys,"
he continued. "Our own freedom we care about deeply, but
nobody else's. Christ said, 'Let him without sin cast the first
stone.' And here we've gone and become the first-stone spe-
cialists of the whole human race."

"Now, wait a minute, Jack," O'Toole said, a belligerent
note creeping into his voice.

"Yeah," Chuck McDermott said. "Enough o' that blarney.
Listen, Mike, why don't you sing us that nutty song you
used to do. You know. It starts 'Oh, she was a pretty child.' "

"Oh, yeah," Mike said, and started right in, without waiting for O'Toole's harmonica:

> "Oh, she was a pretty child
>   And she drove the fellas wild
>   But if anybody tried to make a pass,
>   Well, she was an awful flirt
>   But she'd never lift her skirt
>   So how-in-the-hell could we ever see her—
>   Aaauunnt Matilda was the old lady's name."

Even Jack had to laugh.

142

CHAPTER SIX

In the dining room, David said to his mother, "What did you do when Daddy died? Who did you leave me with?"

"Well, to go back a little," his mother said, "after the little girl agreed to take care of you, I went to the Catholic church there and a priest promised me to see your father in the hospital, which he did, and gave him the last rites of the Church. When your father died in my arms I thought we were all alone, see, but that dear couple were right there and offered to do anything and everything for me. They were just strangers. The manager of Loew's Theatre was there, too, and he offered every help. He asked if Billy had belonged to any orders or clubs. I said the Elks, so he said he'd take me to the local Elks Hall. When we got back to the hotel we had a hard time getting into the room because the door was locked from the inside. You were hollering like mad."

"Belle," Margaret said, "is it a good idea to go through all this?"

"Why not?" Belle said. "He asked. He wants to know."

"Was I all alone?" David asked, hoping the conversation would never stop.

"No," his mother said, "but the little colored girl was dead asleep or passed out, one or the other. Anyway, the manager called and said he'd pick me up the next morning to take me to the Elks, which he did. Before we left the manager's office, it's funny, I was looking at a paper on the desk with a headline saying, 'Lest We Forget,'—as if I ever could. So, anyway, we went to the office of the head of the Elks in Atlanta. The manager introduced me and *Mr. Big* immediately went into a raging tirade saying, 'The Elks are not going to give these actors *one cent*,' and on and on like that. Well, *baby*, that's all I needed. I said, 'Listen, buster, I didn't *ask* for anything. Our manager just thought there was some service the Elks would do to pay respects to a dead member.' Well, he ignored me and started screaming again saying, 'And you're not going to take that body out of this town until you pay the doctor, the hospital and the undertaker.' So our manager interrupted and said, 'Listen, mister, actors don't *beg*, they *give*.' He really told him off good and then we left. Our manager must have wired E. F. Albee about it all, and Albee immediately wired back a thousand dollars' insurance from the NVA."

"The what?"

"The National Vaudeville Artists. It was like an actor's union. But it all caused delay, and you and I sat all day long in the depot . . . with the box your father's body was in right under our eyes."

"I wish I could remember," David said.

"You were too young. Now I have to go back. When Billy was taken to the hospital I wired Mrs.—your grandma— thinking she might want to see him, or at least I felt I owed

it to Billy to let her know. No answering wire from the old
bat, but after three days a letter came saying it was too bad
he was sick and if he wanted to come home they guessed
they could find a place for him. Well, after the Elks making
me miss my scheduled train, and causing our long wait all
those hours in the depot, I got to thinking of how hard-
hearted the Considines were—they were *north* of Ireland, you
know—and what with exhaustion and worry and rage, I sent
them a wire saying Billy was dead and I was taking his body
to Chicago, but that I wouldn't bury him from their home.
Or from yours, Maggie. You and me were on the outs at the
time."

"I remember," Margaret said. "Belle, shouldn't Davey go
to sleep?"

"I'm just telling him this story to *put* him to sleep. So,
anyway, May Mulcahey offered to bury him from *their* place,
but I said I'd bury him from Kenny's undertaking rooms. So,
when we arrived in Chicago, lo and behold, the Considines
and you, Maggie, and poor Ma were at the depot all crying and talking at once. You were saying, 'Oh, Belle, please
don't hurt his poor mother,' and so on."

"I remember that," Margaret said. "May had called me with
all the news. The Considines—your Aunt Hilda doing the
talking, Davey, started to lay your mother out, and how!
Well, you know me, I put Hilda in her place and fast."

"Right," Belle said, "but I was too tired to fight, so I al-
lowed them to take the body to Mrs. Considine's. I remember,
Hughie Kenny and I had to go to Mount Olivet Cemetery
to buy a burial lot. Mrs. Considine asked me to buy a lot for

them, too. So I bought and paid for an eight-grave lot for *our* family and a four-grave lot for them. That meant a grave for your Uncle Herbert, too, although he was a Mason. Mrs. Considine paid 350 dollars (after) for a lovely bench with a heavy stone base that they put under a nice tree between the two lots. The bench, stone base and all, vanished a long time ago. If there's no honor among thieves, there ain't much among the cemetery people either."

"I think he's fallen asleep, Belle, God bless him."

"Yeah," Belle said, "I guess he has." The women tiptoed out, after tucking David's blanket in and turning off a lamp on a nearby table. They walked to the parlor and again stood quietly by the casket, looking down at their mother.

"Belle, doesn't she look beautiful?"

"Beautiful, God love her."

"Do you think she'll run into Dada in the next world?"

"Well, if she did," Belle said, "and if I was her—I'd give him hell."

Margaret gave her the high sign that others were present. "Oh, Sarah," she said, "would you be interested in another nice, hot cup of tea, and maybe another sandwich?"

"Oh, no thank you, Maggie," Sarah McCaffrey said, "but we'll be running along any minute now." They had been saying it all day but had not the slightest interest in doing it.

"That's right, Marge," Mary McCaffrey said, "we do have to be running along."

"Well," Margaret said, "it's been good of yez to stay as long as you have, believe me."

"You know," Sarah said, "there's plenty who was here

today, in and out like butterflies visitin' a rosebush, but, as I was just saying to Mary, we haven't too much time left on this earth ourselves, and, of course, none of us know when we might go, like that. And when Mary or me are lyin' there like your dear mother is now—God bless her—well, it'll be wonderful to know that there are those who care enough to spend not just a few minutes, but a few hours with us."

"Yes," Mary said, "and to say for our departed souls not just a 'Hail, Mary' and a 'Glory Be,' but the full rosary, and that not once, but two or three times at least. We were just on the third of the five *sorrowful* mysteries when you came in."

"Well, that's very generous of you both, Mary," Belle said.

"Make yourselves at home then," Margaret said. "Are you hungry, Belle?"

"I could go for another ham sandwich, I think," her sister said.

"Come on," Margaret said. They headed for the kitchen.

"How are the sandwiches holding out?" Margaret said to Jack.

"Fine," he said. "There's plenty left. And Josie was kind enough to go out and get some nice fresh coffeecake." Josephine was eating a piece of pastry and drinking coffee. She smiled at Jack.

"And I see she's kind enough to eat it herself," Belle said half jokingly.

"Now, Belle," Margaret said, feeling vague alarm. Mike slammed down his cup angrily.

"I'm just *kidding*, Maggie," Belle said. "My God, can't anyone in this family take a joke?"

"Jokes we can take, Belle," Jack said, "but not much else. Is Davey-boy asleep?"

"Yes."

"You can be proud of him, Belle," Jack said. "He's a good boy."

"And Maggie, *you* deserve a lot of the credit for it," Josie said.

"Oh, she does, does she?" Belle said, turning.

"No, he's your son, Belle," Margaret cut in, "and whatever way he is now, that's the way he was born."

"I didn't mean anything *wrong*," Josie said, "I just meant—"

"Never mind, Josie," Mike said. "No matter *what* you said, there's some people could turn it around to start trouble." He glared at Belle, who stared back at him in confused desperation. Josie turned on her heel and left the room.

Margaret, making an effort to change the subject, said, "Well, now, I'm sure Tommy and John and all of yez have better things to listen to than this kind of talk. Jack, what . . . uh . . . what have you been doing to keep yourself busy the last few years? Most of the time, I mean. I know you were with that paper in Boston."

"You've never read any of my books, have you, Mag?" Jack said, smiling.

"Well, I read one of 'em. The one with all the different stories."

"And?"

"And what?"

"Good God," he said, laughing, "this family would rather go to its grave than hand out compliments. Maggie, I don't *need* your compliments, but it would be good for *you* if you knew how to give 'em out. Oh, we praise each other, I guess, but never in the way it'd do the most good. Never face to face."

"Well, the stories were all right, Jack," Margaret said, uneasy. "They were fine, in fact. But now that you bring it up, I don't see why they're all so—you know, so *sad*. Didn't we ever have any laughs in the old days?"

"Oh, certainly," he said. "And some time maybe I'll write about them, too. But, you see, Maggie, fellas who write stories for a living—and this goes for the no-talents, as well as the greats—they usually write about *bad* news, not good news. When things are good, we just enjoy them—we live them. We laugh or we kiss or eat or drink or play with our children or whatever. But when we're *unsatisfied* with reality, we want to change it—we want to complain about it—and that's what most writing is all about."

"That's right, Jack," O'Toole said, coming to life. "It's like them songs we was talking about a while ago. There's a place for a lively jig or a reel, but the *sad* songs are the best o' them all."

"The Church herself tells us this is a vale of tears, Maggie," Chuck McDermott said.

"And that's just why we need a smile and a joke and a gay song and a story with a happy ending," Margaret said. "God knows, there's enough sadness to life itself without writing books about it. Why, the stories of yours I did read, Jack, they sound as if they were written by some long-faced Russian Jew. I couldn't see anything Irish about them, if you must know, although the writing was nice."

"Ah, the Jews," Jack said, rising, with a bitter smile. "I was wondering when we'd get around to them."

"You can't avoid 'em these days," John O'Toole said. "They're takin' over half the South Side."

"And where *should* they live, John?" Jack said rather loudly.

"What?"

"The Jews. You don't want 'em here on the South Side, and the Swedes and the Polacks don't want 'em on the North Side. So where, then, you tell me—where *should* they live?"

"Well, in their own neighborhood, for God's sake," O'Toole said. "Anybody knows that."

"Lower your voice, Jack," Belle said. "Poor Ma's not yet in her grave. What are you trying to say, that we're anti-Semitic? We're not. But the Jews did kill Christ, didn't they?"

"No!" Jack shouted. "They did not. We don't know for sure who killed Christ, although I'd put you and me high on the list of suspects, Belle. But He wasn't killed by the *Jews.* 'The Jews' are some twenty million people alive today. Christ was killed by Roman soldiers, urged on by a crowd of maybe two hundred Jews—two thousand years ago. Are you and I responsible for the things that our old man did *twenty* years ago? Are we responsible for what Grandfather Scanlan did, or the other one Ma used to talk about, Great-grandfather McDevitt? Of course not! Well, if not, then what kind of idiocy is it to blame *today's* Jews for a crime of which none of them personally are in any sense guilty?"

"Aw, take it easy, Jack," Mike said. "We're all on the same side. John didn't mean no harm. Nobody's perfect."

"I know," Jack said, "but I can't stand the combination of imperfection and arrogant self-righteousness. It's one of the things that made me fold up my tent at the seminary. I'll tell you something surprising. *I'm* anti-Semitic. Yes! Yes, I'm still a *little* anti-Semitic. I haven't been able to wash it all out of me. But the point is, I'm ashamed of it. You're that way and you're *not* ashamed of it. In fact, you wouldn't give it up for the world, so there's no hope for you. But the funny part of it is, I don't think you even know that it's wrong to be that way. You feel very righteous about it, so maybe you're not even guilty of any wrongdoing in the sight of Heaven, just because you're so Goddamned ignorant. Do you know what's going on in Europe right now? That would really be a laugh. Here you are lousing up the world with your hatred and you don't even know it's wrong—so maybe on that score old St. Pete would let you tiptoe by the pearly gates after all, for all your innocent viciousness."

"Aw, that's pretty strong talk, Jack," Tom Monaghan said good-naturedly. "Have a drink."

"No," Jack said. "I'm just sobering up. The basic problem, Mike—and this goes for you, too, Belle—and Mag—all of you —the basic problem is this . . . that you don't think there's anything seriously *wrong* with you."

"What are ya talkin' about, Jack?" Margaret said. "Good God, don't we keep goin' to confession time after time?"

"I'd like to know the last time *he* went!" Belle said, afraid of Jack, yet unable to hold her tongue.

"Shhh, Belle," Margaret said. "And what do we go for if not to admit that we've sinned?"

"Christ, Mag," Jack said, "*I* know about confession. But I'm telling you, you don't go to confess your *faults*—you go only to confess your *mistakes!*"

"Ain't they the same thing?" Matty Mulcahey asked.

"Not by a damned sight!" Jack snapped. "Ask yourselves —exactly what is it you confess? That you missed Mass on Sunday. That you told a lie. That you took the name of the Lord in vain. That you had an impure thought—which to you probably means *any* thought on *that* subject. What else? That you ate meat on Friday. That you fell off the wagon. That you lost your temper."

"Well, Jeez, Jack," Mike said, "ain't those the things that any normal person would confess?"

"That's penny-ante stuff!" Jack said. "It's almost beside the point. All that business does for you is make you feel good —make you feel all innocent and holy for a few hours— without ever once really stirring up the muddy water and forcing you to look into its depths. Jesus said Know the truth—learn the truth, and it'll make you free. But you don't *want* to know the truth. You don't want to be free. Being free would scare you to death."

"The truth about *what*, for God's sake?" Josie said.

"The truth about yourselves. You see, despite all your confessing and novenas and candles, you're secretly convinced that what's really wrong with the world is what *other* people do. It's not *you*—it's the Jews or the Protestants or the Communists or the 'niggers' or the Dagos or God knows who."

"Oh, I get it," Belle said bitterly. "It's just the Catholics and the Irish who're wrong, is that it?"

"No, Belle, that isn't it. *Everybody's* wrong, part of the time. Your mistake is that you don't realize you're part of everybody. Jeez, they call the Jews God's chosen people, but after what the rest of us have done to them the past two thousand years, I doubt if many of 'em still believe it. But the Irish—they're *certain* they're God's chosen people. I'll prove it to you. First of all, it's obvious that whoever the chosen people are, they're Catholic. I mean, there's only one true Church—right?"

"Well," Mike said, "Christ said on this rock I will build my Church. He didn't say rocks."

"No mistake about that. But who, among all the Catholic nations, is really on the inside track? It can't be the Italians. Don't we know they're a bunch of gangsters or a lot of silly children with their songs and dances and stupid Wop accents? The French, maybe? Not a chance. Why, millions of 'em are atheists, and everybody knows the French are a filthy race who commit excesses of the flesh too disgusting to mention. The very word *French* is a dirty word among us, isn't it? What about the Spaniards? Well, now, nobody's going to argue that a stupid bunch of Spics know anything about religion, for God's sake. Why—don't some of their priests even get married—or worse—and aren't they the most ignorant people you've ever met—fit only to be circus acrobats or tango dancers or prize fighters? No, the Spanish are out. Who's left? The Irish."

He sang loudly, " 'Oh, a little bit of heaven fell . . . from out the sky one day . . .' Ha! Do you know, Maggie, that at this very moment down in Bughouse Square there's a man standing on a box tellin' crowds that the Irish are one of the ten lost tribes of Israel."

John O'Toole slammed his fist on the table, making the glasses and coffee cups dance. "Well Goddamn it," he said. "That's the limit." He rose and moved quickly to Jack, his face reddening. "What are ya sayin' now? That we're all a bunch of Jews?"

"Take it easy, John," Tom Monaghan said.

"Easy, hell," O'Toole said. "Jack, if your poor mother wasn't lyin' in there right now I'd pop you one, I swear to God."

Mike was on his feet. "And if you didn't," he said, "I would, Goddamn it." He was furious with his brother, not just for his criticisms, some of which he had scarcely heard, but for spoiling the party, for turning such a warm, pleasant meeting of old friends into an angry, disturbing inquisition.

"Now, Mike," Margaret said, putting her hand on his arm, "don't start anything."

"Me?" he said. "What the hell am *I* starting? I'm not the one doin' this crazy Communist talk. And another thing, if anybody lays a hand on my brother, it'll be *me*. John, you sit down."

"Who the hell you tellin' to sit down?" O'Toole demanded.

"You," Mike said, pointing at him.

"Aw, will ya keep it quiet," Chuck McDermott said. "This *is* a wake, ya know."

"And if you don't shut up," Mike said, "there'll be another one in about a minute."

"Maggie," John O'Toole shouted, "I'm leavin'. I love you and all the girls in this family, but your brothers never did have any sense."

"Ah, shut up, John," Tom Monaghan said.

"And as I leave this house," O'Toole said to Mike and Jack, "you'll notice a piece o' mistletoe pinned to the tail o' me coat."

Monaghan followed him out, saying, "Mag, Belle, we'll see ya all later. So long, fellas."

Chuck McDermott and Matty Mulcahey rose and fumblingly made their way to the porch door.

"Come on, Matty," Chuck said. "Let's get ta hell outta here."

When the last good-by had been said, sodden silence fell over the kitchen. Belle sighed and said, "Well, you can see what you did, Jack, givin' *him* a drink." She pointed at Mike.

"Never mind, Belle," Margaret said.

"We'll take no advice about drinkin' from the likes of you, Belle," Mike said.

"Ah, Mike, leave her alone," Jack said. "Don't take it out on her."

"Can't you just all *stop?*" Margaret said. "Think of poor Ma. Haven't you any respect for the dead?"

"Oh, we've got plenty of that, sister," Jack said. "Our problem is we haven't enough respect for the *living*."

Belle glared at him. "What's that supposed to mean?"

"It means," he said, "that Ma's generation is gone and ours is over the hill. But what are you goin' to do about little Davey in there?"

"Oh, it's that again, is it?" Belle said. "Well, I won't listen to any more of this."

She ran out, followed by Margaret.

In the kitchen there was a long pause.

"I'm sorry about all that big talk," Jack said, quietly.

"Forget it," Mike said. "You might even be right . . . about one thing or another."

"Ya know, Mike, I wish all of us were creatures of *my* imagination, instead of God's. If this were all just one of *my* stories now, why it'd be the easiest thing in the world to put a happy ending on it, for all of us. *You'd* stop drinking —for good—and get yourself a decent job. And *keep* it. And Rose and her husband would stop fightin' and live happily ever after, and maybe have a child instead of a dog. And Josie would go back to California and live in peace with her own family. And Maggie'd stop havin' to walk from one end of downtown Chicago to the other collectin' bills for the Railway Express and retire with a nice comfortable pension. And Belle would come to her senses and settle down somehow and make a decent home for little Dave."

"And what about yourself, Jack?" Mike said.

"Me? Oh, I don't know. Maybe I'd stop writin' *second-rate* books and turn out something really worthwhile, and maybe get a job in Paris for one of the Boston or New York papers."

"That'd all be nice, all right," Mike said, looking at his scarred knuckles.

"But the thing is, brother, when it comes to writin' nice easy plot lines the Almighty has no class at all. The power is out of my hands, and all I can see for us is . . . more of the same, and God help the next generation."

"Ow! Ow, no! Don't! You can't be any . . ."

"What's that?" Josie called.

"Is it Davey?" his mother said, hurrying to his cot.

Margaret, too, rushed to David's cot and leaned over him, rubbing his head gently. "That's all right, honey. That's Aunt Maggie's good boy. Was he having a nightmare? Yes. That's a good boy. We're all right here. Everything's fine."

"That child shouldn't be sleeping in there anyway," Josie said, from down the hall.

"What?" Belle said.

"He ought to be in a bedroom," Josie said.

"Well, dammit, he's only sleeping where he is, like a gypsy in a field—because of *you!*" Belle said.

"Me?" Josie said, louder and afraid.

"Yes, you. You're taking his bed tonight, so he *has* to sleep where he is."

"I am *not* taking his bed. Where are *you* going to sleep?"

"I'm not," Belle said. "I'm staying up all night because there's not enough room for me around here. Why? Because of *you.* Sitting up all night is fine for me because I'm not used to much better. But you—the great lady—lady, my ass—"

At that, Sarah McCaffrey, listening in the parlor, leaped to her feet.

"We really must be running along, Josie," she called. "Come, Mary."

"Yes, Sarah." The two women approached the door but did not quite leave.

"What's the *matter*?" Margaret demanded wearily.

"Matter?" Josie said. "You tell this slut to keep a civil tongue in her head, Maggie, or as God is my judge, I'll—"

"You'll *what*, you fat slob!" Belle said, with a sneer. "Oh, don't worry. You'll have your good night's sleep, and I hope it does you a lot of good."

"Belle," Margaret said, "don't do anything foolish. For Davey's sake. For poor Ma's sake! Don't fight."

"All right," Josie said. "I wouldn't waste my time fighting with the likes of her."

"Maggie," Sarah McCaffrey said, "I think we should be running along."

"Yes," Margaret said. "I suppose you *should*, Mary. And Sarah. Thank you so much for staying as long as you did." She ushered the two women out at last. "Good night. Thank you. Good night."

Belle had run to a bedroom while Josie stomped into the parlor. Margaret seated herself absent-mindedly at the foot of David's bed and dabbed at her eyes with a handkerchief. Then she rose and walked to her mother's coffin. Once again she stared lovingly down at the old, careworn face. Looking up at the ancient, faded framed picture of the Sacred Heart she whispered, "Sweet Jesus, help us."

At that moment Jack entered the room, from the kitchen. He paused as he heard his sister say, "Good-by, Ma. I love you."

When she had risen and walked toward him he took her hand in his, in an uncharacteristic gesture of affection, and smiled at her sadly. She seemed surprised at his sudden intimacy and drew away, as if confused and distracted, then went to her room, dabbing at her eyes.

Jack stared after her for a long moment, wondering what it was that pulled her forward daily through life. She had never married and he would not have been surprised to learn that she had never been seriously in love. Such love as she could feel had always been reserved for the members of the family, for her mother and father, her sisters and brothers, and her nephew. She had been no more gifted than the rest at expressing her softer emotions.

At contemplation of her fate, past and future, Jack suddenly clasped his hands together and sighed deeply. Then he spoke silently to himself, "I am holding my left hand with my right because at this moment I must hold somebody's hand."

Turning, he inhaled the aroma of flowers and hot candle wax again, then moved to the coffin and looked down once more at his mother's face. Soon, he knew, there would come a look at her that would be his last.

After a moment he realized that Mike had walked in and was standing behind him.

"Oh, there ya are," Mike said quietly.

"Ah, Mike," Jack said. "I've discovered something about this family. Something fantastic."

"Well, why in the name of Christ don't you just tell us what it *is*," Mike said, "so we can all go to *bed*." He seated himself in an old rocking chair.

"You wouldn't understand," Jack said.

"Well, since there's nobody here now but you and me, you don't need to be troublin' yourself about the rest of 'em. So go ahead. What's wrong with us?"

"How did you know I was going to talk about what's wrong?" Jack said.

"Just by the look on your stupid face, I guess," Mike said. "You never could play stud without tippin' your hand. So go ahead."

"I can't."

"Well, then, maybe it's because we're not such a damned poor bunch after all! We ain't perfect, but there's plenty who are a lot worse. So we drink—all of us except Maggie and Josie, anyway. So what?"

"Did you ever ask yourself *why*, Mike? *Why* we drink? Why we can't live with each other or *without* each other? Why Ma and the old man had twelve of us, but the whole lot of us only produced three for the next generation, and not one of *them* named Scanlan!"

"Well, Christ, Jack—you're a great one to talk. First you head for the priesthood, then you louse that up. And you never got married. How the hell could you—or me—have any kids?"

"Not *how*, Mike. I tell you again the important question

is *why* we didn't. Why Maggie never got married. Why Rose and Charlie O'Brian never had a kid. And why, when Belle had one, she's left him behind from the very first, like a dog you leave in a kennel when you go on the road."

"Well, to hell with Belle. Look what kind she hooks up with when she does find herself a man. But Maggie could've gotten married. Freddie Slater hung around here many a Sunday afternoon and he was interested in something besides free corn beef and cabbage."

"You poor, stupid—don't you see!!? No! Maggie could *never* have gotten married! You and I wouldn't let her. Before he died Joe wouldn't let her. Sure, before Freddie Slater there was Dan Sullivan, and before him—when we lived over near 47th—there was the guy she worked with down at the American Express—but we scared the hell out of all of 'em and they went away. Josie escaped only by running off to California, workin' at Fred Harvey's and hiding from us! And Josie didn't marry Eddie because she *loved* him! She loved Bill Maguire, but you and Joe beat him up that night he brought her home with a few beers in her. She married poor Eddie for *spite!*"

"To spite who?" Mike said, alarmed and puzzled.

"To spite you—me—Joe—the old man—this whole God-damned family!"

"Ah, that's a lie!" Mike said sarcastically. "And besides—the girls have a lot to complain about. Didn't they go after that German woman you was livin' with in St. Louis—that Frieda or Hilda or whatever the hell her name was? Didn't they help you get rid o' her?"

"Oh, yes," Jack said sadly. "But it never occurred to anybody to ask if I *wanted* to get rid of her."

"Didn't you?"

"No, as a matter of fact, I loved that woman. I wanted to marry her."

"Well, why didn't you?"

"I was afraid."

"Of what?"

"I don't know. I don't really know. But I know now that our strange misdeeds, Mike, are not as incomprehensible as they once seemed. They can be understood."

"It's funny, Jack," Mike said quietly, "your sayin' you was afraid. I never thought of you bein' afraid of anything, chief. I knew *I* always was, Goddamn it. But after the old man left I always looked up to you for strength."

"That's a hot one," Jack said, feeling a strange, muffled love for his brother.

"No, I mean it. Oh, you know, I didn't think you were Black Jack Pershing or anything, but compared to the rest of us you had a lot of savvy. And then, you know, your studyin' for the priesthood and all. You were the rock of Gibraltar." He sipped his drink. "Listen, do you want to hear something really goofy?"

"What?"

"Between you and me and the lamppost," Mike said, "I'm glad ya went AWOL at the seminary."

"Why?"

"Well, Jeez, it's tough enough for us in this family to talk to each other straight from the shoulder as it is. If you was

a priest . . . well, hell, I'd have to be cold sober right now
and mindin' my P's and Q's every inch of the way, ya see?
We couldn't be sharin' a drink or shootin' the bull at all. I
mean, even if he's your own brother ya can't go up to a priest
and say, 'Hi ya, Father. How they hangin'?'—ya know?"

Jack laughed. "Well," he said, "I'm sorry to let you down,
little brother, but I'm only human. My only superiority over
the rest of the sons of bitches in this world is that I *admit*
I'm one. God, that *is* goofy. All these years you seein' me as
strong . . . when I didn't see it that way at all. There were
some at St. Leo's with me who were in no better shape but
who stuck it out . . . who went ahead into the priesthood
anyway. Some of them did it because they were right for the
job. Others were like soldiers goin' over the top. They wanted
to back out but it took more guts to do that than to keep in
step."

"How come you quit? I never really knew."

"Because I wasn't enough of a lover," Jack said, looking
at his shoes.

"I don't getcha'."

"I went in for the wrong reasons. I saw early in the game
that this world will break your heart, that it's tough and
cold and that we move daily through evil and rottenness. I
wanted to do something to *stop* all that, isn't that pitiful? I
thought I could put on the collar and preach one great
magical, miraculous sermon that would shake up the world,
put the fear of God into their hearts, and make men fall to
their knees and say *mea culpa, mea culpa—*" he pounded his
breast in a gesture of penitence, "and sin no more. What a

chump! What my conniving heart *really* wanted to be was a dragon slayer. Which is to say—a *copper*, with a *gun* and a *billy* and a *rubber hose!* It's the oldest puzzle on earth, little brother. Do we change this world with a fist or a handshake—with a sword or a kiss—with violence or with love?" He leaned over his brother.

"Love?"

"The very word embarrasses you, doesn't it? It embarrasses me. This Goddamned family can say it loves a pet dog, or it loves an ice-cream soda. But there isn't one of us who can look the other in the eye and say, 'Brother—or sister—I love you!' We are gifted at violence. We stand guard. We avenge. We have no gift for love. When I saw that in the mirror I ran out of the seminary. I've been running ever since." Suddenly he wept and threw himself into a chair.

Mike stood and put his hand on his brother's shoulder. "Aw, listen, Jack. I could say that, old-timer. I . . ." He tried to say 'love'—but the sound would not come out. He punched Jack's arm in a gesture of affectionate helplessness.

In the front bedroom Belle confessed to Rose that she had slipped out of the kitchen with what was left of the bottle of Dago Red. They shared the contents, drinking out of the bottle because there were no glasses in the room except for one filled with water and a pair of false teeth, after which each of them put little black squares of Sen-Sen into their mouths and exhaled heartily to try to remove the smell of wine from their breaths.

After a few minutes the alcohol relaxed them and they began to speak in louder tones, to reminisce, and to laugh.

"Belle," Rose said, "do you remember the time when Irish gangsters killed Cronin, that big cop, I forget what his first name was, and it was in all the papers the week Ma had that terrible fight with the Jew woman in Walgreen's drugstore?"

"Oh, God, yeah," Belle said, laughing. "Ma, who never got mad at anybody, lost her temper and said to the woman, 'Aah, who killed Christ?' and the woman said, 'Yeah? Who killed *Cronin?*'"

They both laughed so hard, remembering, that their kidneys hurt. Suddenly Josie burst out of the next room, followed by Margaret.

"Now, Josie," Maggie said, "don't start anything."

"Never mind," Josie said. "I'm entitled to a little sleep around here, ain't I?" She opened the door down the hall and looked in angrily at Belle and Rose.

"What the hell do *you* want?" Belle said, at the expression on her face.

"I just want a little quiet around here, that's all," Josie said.

"Then lower your own voice," Rose said.

"Don't you talk to me like that, Rosie," Josie said. "I'm not askin' for any favors. I'm just dead tired from travelin' two thousand miles to get here and I don't have to put up with all this drinkin' and carousin' in here from you two!"

"Goddamn it," Belle said. "That's the limit." In jumping up off the bed she bumped into a side table and knocked it down. They all winced and shied like sensitive cattle at the sound of crashing glass.

"Now look what you've done!" Josie cried. "Breakin' Ma's things." Belle had reached over to pick up a broken button box when Josie's attack suddenly pushed her to fury. She raised the object in a threatening gesture.

"Just you try it," Josie said. Belle threw the box blindly. It hit the wall and Josie backed out of the room.

"Now see what you've done," Margaret said to Josie. "I told you not to go in there."

"What *I've* done?" Josie shouted. "It's not me! It's that whore."

"That does it," Belle shouted, rushing out past them, through the hallway and into the parlor. "I'm getting out of here."

"What the hell's wrong now?" Mike said.

"Mike," Rose said, "Belle's leaving."

"You're Goddamned right I am," Belle said. "I don't have to stay around here and take any abuse from that big slob."

"Belle, sshh," Margaret said, "Davey'll hear you."

"She doesn't care," Josie said. "Listen, Maggie, you tell this slut to keep a civil tongue in her head or as God is my judge I'll—"

"You'll what?" Belle cried, her face a mask of contempt. "Come on, you'll what?"

Josie glared at her but did not speak.

"Come on, Davey. Wake up." Belle's voice was getting even louder. She hurried to his cot and shook him.

"Belle," Margaret said, "come into the parlor, please. Better poor Ma's ears hear all this than the ears of that child."

"Never mind," Belle said. "Josie, this isn't the first time you ran me out of my mother's house but by God it'll be the last."

Josie snorted and turned her back.

"Belle," Jack said, "don't talk foolish."

"Sure," Belle said. "That's it. Side with her. That's the way it's always been around here. You and Maggie and Josie —the 'sensible' ones—against me and Rosie."

"Shut up in front of Ma," Mike said, in his frustration unable to make any more rational contribution to the argument.

"Oh, don't worry, Mike," Belle shouted, on the verge of tears. "Ma'll have peace and quiet in the grave. And it'll get pretty Goddamned quiet here before I set foot in this house again."

"Jesus," Jack said. "What's the matter *now?*"

"I wish I knew," Margaret said, pacing back and forth.

"Tell 'em, Josie," Belle said. "Tell 'em I've never been able to make a move to satisfy you—or *any* of you, for the last forty years. I was *Ma's* favorite, though, by God—for all my sins—and you were all jealous of that."

"Belle, shut up!" Mike said, clenching his fists, bewildered.

"You *try* and shut me up! And why should you, Mike? You and me—the two black sheep—we were Ma's two favorites."

"Belle, you poor silly woman," Jack said, "don't you realize that's all that this cursed family produced was black sheep? And with the rest of the sheep we're headed for the slaughter-house."

"Listen, Jack," Josie said, "don't be callin' me and Maggie black sheep. It's Belle we were talkin' about. It's no wonder that Dada left home and poor Ma is in her grave with the worry *she* caused 'em."

"Josie," Rose said, "you can't blame Belle for Ma's death. Every one of us added a nail to her coffin."

"Me?" Josie shouted. "What the hell did *I* do to kill Ma?"

"You ran away as early as you could and you stayed away. As soon as you saved up enough money from the shoe factory you went and got that job waitin' on table at the Fred Harvey. You ran as far as you were able, till the Pacific Ocean wouldn't let you run any farther. You were never here to help Ma, so don't hand us that."

"Rose, for God's sake, shut up," Jack said. "We all ran off one way or another. None of us but Maggie ever stayed with Ma."

"But I was right here in this town," Rose said, turning to Belle. "I saw Ma a lot. Didn't I, Belle?"

"Yes, Rose, you did," Belle said. "The only reason *I* had to leave was first because there was no peace in this town, and second, to keep from starvin' to death."

"To keep Billy Considine and Doug Roberts from starvin' to death, you mean!" Josie said.

"You foul-mouthed bitch," Belle said, lunging at her. "I'll kill you." Mike stepped in and grabbed her wrists as she lifted her arms.

"Belle!" Jack shouted. "Sister, stop it!"

"Ah, let her go," Josie said, standing defiantly, her clenched fists on her hips.

Belle stepped back, wrenching her arms free from Mike.

"She can't talk to me like that and get away with it," she

shouted, her eyes wild and sad. "Half of every Goddamned ten-, twenty-, fifty- and hundred-dollar bill I ever sent to this house—and by God I've sent plenty—half of that money belonged to Billy Considine or Doug Roberts!"

"Shut up, Belle," Mike said, sneering at her strangely. "We don't want to hear about Doug Roberts. His name means nothing in this house. And Bill Considine meant nothing except that he was little Dave's father. At least you *married* that one."

"Why, you—" She tried to slap him, but he grabbed her arms.

"Let me go!" she shouted, drawing away.

"And good riddance," Josie cried. "We don't want whores in this house."

"Josie, my God," Margaret said. "Can't you see *David* sitting right there? Do you want him to hear all this? Belle, wait."

"Let me go," Belle shouted. "I should have known better than to come into this house again." She was running to David, her eyes like those of a frightened horse. "David," she said. "Didn't you hear me before? Come on, get up!"

"Belle," Mag said, "the child needs his sleep."

"Did Josie think of that when she came barging into our room?" Belle said, pulling back the bedclothes that covered David.

"What's the matter, Mama?" he said.

"Never mind, Davey," his mother said. "Just get up and get dressed. We're not welcome here."

"Belle," Margaret said, shaking her head. "That's not true.

No matter how you hate the rest of us, don't do this. Don't use this child as a weapon. Think of what you're doing!"

"Leave me alone," Belle said. "He's mine, isn't he? Rosie, help me find and pack his clothes."

"Is somebody drunk?" David asked, rubbing his eyes sleepily.

"There, you see?" Belle said. "You see what the child learns in this house?" She ran in and out of a bedroom, bringing a shirt and trousers for David. "Here, put these on, and hurry." He started to dress. "Rose, gimme that old brown suitcase."

Rose produced the suitcase from a bedroom.

"Belle," she said, "don't you think you ought to let poor David get a good night's sleep? Whatever you want to do can be done just as well tomorrow."

Belle shouted, a note of triumph in her voice. "Oh, no, and don't *you* side with them, Rosie. I know what they're up to. Turning the child against me so every year he's more of a stranger. Leave him here? Not on your life! This is where he hears that I'm no good, that I'm a drunk, that I'm a dope fiend, that I'm—"

"Honey," Margaret said, "don't worry about what your mama is saying, she's just angry. Tomorrow she'll be sorry, you'll see."

"No, Maggie," Belle said, handing David a pair of socks, "tomorrow *you'll* be sorry. I'm taking my child away from you so fast it'll make your head swim! Hurry up, Davey!"

She ran into the bedroom for more clothes, then got her own coat and hat.

David, who up to now had been first frightened by the angry passion that flickered about him, like invisible lightning, then confused about the reason for the argument, suddenly, clearly grasped the idea that his mother was taking him away with her after all. His heart leaped up.

"Mama," he said, "are you really gonna take me with you? Oh, boy! Don't worry, Aunt Maggie, it's all right. Mama's gonna take me with her, like she used to. Maybe we'll go to California again." He continued dressing quickly.

"Oh, Davey," Margaret said, embracing him.

"I'll write to you every day, Aunt Mag. See? Everything worked out after all. Mama won't stay mad. She'll bring me back to visit real soon, you'll see. Don't worry."

"Jack," Margaret said, while Belle was out of the room, "isn't there anything we can do to—?"

"No," he said, "there isn't."

"The boy belongs to Belle," Mike said, looking pale.

"That's all right, Uncle Mike," Davey said as he pulled on a sweater, "I'll write to *you* too and let you know what towns we're in and everything. Gosh, maybe we'll go to the Hotel Sherman tonight and I can have all the cocoa I want."

Belle returned, carrying a large shopping bag full of clothes, and a suitcase. "That's all I can carry for now. I'll send a cab for his bike and the rest of his clothes later. We'll go downtown on the streetcar."

"You want me to call for a taxi, Belle?" Rose said.

"No," Belle said, "whatever's to be done, I'll do it myself. Davey, it's a long ride downtown. Go to the toilet before we leave. And comb your hair."

"Okay," he said cheerfully, and hurried into the bathroom.

"Where the hell did I leave Nellie Riley's phone number?" Belle said, looking through her purse.

"Belle," Margaret said, feeling all at once very cold, "I thought *you* were going to take him!"

"Never mind," Belle said, fumbling with powder puffs, lipstick, coins, hairpins and rubber bands in her pocketbook.

"Belle, listen," Margaret said, "you can't do this. You can't take him away from me like this. He's the only child I ever had. I'll never have one of my own."

"Oh, here's the number," Belle said.

"Ah, God," Mag said. "Belle, for Davey's sake. For Ma's sake. *Look* at her, Belle. Look at her lyin' in there. She never knew three full days' peace in a row in her whole life. Are you going to do this to her now? Aren't you even going to let her go to her grave in peace?" She hurried up and down in the room, wringing her hands, tears filling her eyes.

"Oh, Jesus, Mary and Joseph," she said. "You're all driving me crazy. I'm not asking for much. You'll be gone soon anyway, Belle. But for that child's sake—"

But as she spoke Belle had lifted the phone and jiggled the receiver. "Operator," she said, "give me Morgan 8264."

"Is that Morgan 8264?" the operator said.

"Yes."

"Thank you."

When the number had rung twice, Nellie Riley picked up her phone.

"Hello?"

"Hello, Nellie?"

"Yes?"

"It's me, Belle. I hope I didn't wake you."

"No," Nellie said, "we're still up. What's wrong?"

"Listen, Nellie," Belle said, "remember this afternoon when you said if ever I was in a spot you'd take little David in as a boarder?"

"Oh, Belle, I'm sorry," Nellie said. "Is it the trouble you were expecting?"

"Listen, Belle," Rose cut in, "if it's just a matter of a week or so, Charlie and I would be glad to—"

"Shut up a minute, Rose," Belle said.

"Well, sure, Belle," Nellie was saying, "I meant every word I said. We'll be glad to have David stay with us."

"That's wonderful," Belle said. "You're a real pal."

"Well, my God, Belle, what are friends for? But what happened?"

"Oh, you know," Belle said. "You could see it coming this afternoon, couldn't ya?"

"Well, I don't know, Belle," Nellie said. "I honestly didn't."

"Well, I sure as hell did," Belle said. "Well, listen, I can't talk any more now. I'm goin' to a hotel tonight and then I'll get out to your place tomorrow somehow. Now you understand I'm talking about *payin'*, not moochin' on ya."

"Belle, I wouldn't hear of it," Nellie said. "Little Davey'll be good company for Frank, Junior."

"I know, Nellie, but either I pay you or it's no dice. What do you say to five hundred dollars for a whole year, room and board?"

Mike jumped up and approached her. "Belle," he said, "a year is a long time, especially for a kid."

"Well," Nellie said, "you just come right on over here whenever you want to, even tonight if you want, and we can talk everything over. It'll be fine, either way."

"Okay, Nellie. Thanks for everything. So long."

"Belle, my God," Margaret said, when her sister had hung up, "don't put that boy in with strangers."

"Listen, Maggie," Belle said softly, "I'd-a been dead a long time ago if it wasn't for strangers."

David ran back to the room with his cap on but took it off quickly. "Is my hair all right, Mama Belle?" he said.

"Yeah, fine," she answered. "Come on." She picked up her suitcase and moved toward the front door.

"Wait a minute, Mama," David said. He ran back down the hall and Margaret embraced him, kissing him on the top of the head, then on the face, trying to smile. Jack and Mike walked over to him, pursing their lips, trying to appear calm.

"So long, old-timer," Jack said. "Take care of yourself, champ."

"Yeah," Mike said. "Keep your left up and your chin down, pardner."

"Okay," David said. "I will. It's nice to have seen ya again, Uncle Jack. Aunt Maggie, thanks for letting Mama take me. When we come back from California I'll come and visit you. You'll see. Real soon. Don't cry. And I'll write to all of you." He gave Aunt Rose a kiss as she hugged him.

"Davey," Jack said, "do me a favor, will ya? Wait in here

for just a minute. I want to go out and say something to your mother."

Belle stepped out of the apartment, down the carpeted steps of the vestibule, and out into the chill night air. Jack followed her.

"Listen, Belle," he said, "you know what you're doing, don't you? I mean, I don't blame you for losin' your temper and all, but is that all there is to this thing?"

"What do you mean?" she said warily.

"Well," he said, pausing momentarily, "there's something I thought you and I would never discuss, but I've got to bring it up. Forgive me."

"What the hell are you talking about?" she said. "It's getting late."

"Sister," Jack said, speaking in a softer tone and moving away from the front window of the apartment so that nothing he said could be heard inside, "are you sure this isn't Alabama all over again?"

She stood stock-still and silent in front of him, her mouth open. Then she made a strange soft sound, almost like a growl.

"What the hell are you talking about?" she said at last.

"Belle, let's not kid around. I know about what happened in Mobile, Alabama."

"Why," she said, "what do you mean? *Nothing* happened in Mobile, Alabama."

"Belle," he said, "cut the crap. I said I *know*."

"How do you know?" she said. "What do you know?"

"You thought only Rosie knew, but she told me when the

thing first happened. She thought maybe I could talk you out of it. But by the time I heard about it, the thing was over and done with."

"I don't know what the hell Rosie *told* you but I never—"

"Are you deaf?" he shouted. "I know. I know about *Edwin*. I know that you had him out of wedlock and that when he was four years old you just gave him away one day, like you'd give away a dog."

"Oh," she said, turning her head back and forth very slowly again and again, her eyes getting wider. "Oh, you son of a bitch. You son of a bitch. Who the hell do you think you are, throwing this in my face? Leave me alone."

"Listen, Belle," he said, "I didn't bring the thing up for its own sake. I never knew who the father was, or how or why it happened, or any of that. I never knew Edwin and it was all none of my business. I just felt sorry for you, was all, and I wished that I could have helped you somehow, when it was all happening."

"You son of a bitch," she said again, softly, seeming not to hear him now. "Get away from me." She backed up on the sidewalk.

"The only reason I bring the thing up now—don't worry, Rosie and I are the only ones who know about it—Ma never knew—the only reason I bring it up now is to *warn* you, before you do the same thing with Davey that you did with the other one."

"What the hell was I supposed to do with the other one?" she said, still backing away in horror. "Bring him home to *this* house, to *this* family? With no husband? You can see how they treat me already. What do you think my life would have been if I brought a kid like that home?"

"But think of *now*," he said. "What's done is done, but it doesn't have to happen to Davey."

"What the hell do you think happened to the other one? That he was thrown into a garbage dump? Given to gypsies? No, I gave him to a good family and he's been raised in good boarding schools, down South."

"With strangers."

"I've got to go," she said. "I don't want to miss the next streetcar."

He sighed, shook his head and walked back into the building.

"Come on, Davey-boy," he said. "Your mother is waiting for you."

"Okay, Uncle Jack," David said, running delirious with joy, down the steps and out to the nighttime city and the wide, waiting world.

When he saw his mother standing under the nearby street lamp, looking away from him, but waiting for him, he threw back his head and shouted, "California, here I come!"